So Much
to Tell You

Lothian YA Fiction

JOHN MARSDEN

So Much to Tell You

Lothian
BOOKS

To
John Mazur,
the 'Lindell' of this book;
and to
'Lisa'

Thomas C. Lothian Pty Ltd
132 Albert Road, South Melbourne, Victoria 3205

First published 1987 by Walter McVitty Books. Paperback edition
first published 1988, reprinted 1988, 1989 (three times), 1990 (twice),
1991 (three times), 1992 (twice), 1993 (twice), 1994, 1995,
2nd paperback edition 1995, reprinted 1996, 1997.
Paperback reprint first published by
Thomas C. Lothian Pty Ltd 1997.
Reprinted 1998, 1999
This paperback edition first published 1999
Reprinted 2000, 2001, 2002

National Library of Australia
Cataloguing-in-Publication data:

Marsden, John, 1950–

So much to tell you.

ISBN 0 85091 941 X.

A823.3

Printed in Australia by Griffin Press

February 6

I don't know what I am doing here.

Well, I do really. It's because I was getting nowhere at the hospital. I have been sent here to learn to talk again. Sent here because my mother can't stand my silent presence at home. Sent here because of my face, I suppose. I don't know.

This is my third day at this boarding school, Warrington, but today was the first day of classes. Mr Lindell, our English teacher, gave us these journals and told us we have to write in them every night, during homework (except that homework here is called Prep). We have Prep every weeknight, for two hours a night. For that time we have to sit at our desks and be silent. This would suit me were it true but of course it isn't ... people whisper, talk, pass messages, exclaim out loud when they make a mistake. They do not whisper or pass messages to me, and the words break over my desk in soft waves, white foam washing around me.

I am in Prep now, writing this at my desk. On my left is a girl called Cathy Preshill. On the right is a girl called Sophie Smith. Cathy seems very thin to me and I wonder if she has anorexia, but she probably doesn't. *I* do though — anorexia of speech.

This journal is starting to scare me already. When Mr Lindell gave them out in class I felt the fear and promised myself that I would not write in it, that it would stay a cold and empty book, with no secrets. Now here I am on the first page saying more than I wanted to, more than I should. What if he reads them? He said he wouldn't; that we were free to write almost anything and that he would glance through them once in a while to make sure we were using them, not just filling them with swear words. If he doesn't keep his promise I am lost.

February 8

Today is Friday, tomorrow is Saturday.

Saturday and Sunday together make up the weekend.

I did not write in this journal yesterday. Will I get into trouble for that, I wonder?

Yesterday we had tennis practice. It is compulsory to go if tennis is your sport and, as tennis is my sport, I went. But I sat under a tree outside the court and watched. Watched all the tennis players laughing and hitting shots and missing shots. When they miss easy shots they giggle, turn to their partners, go red (the red of giggling more than the red of embarrassment), bend a little at the knees and drop their hands to around the level of their kneecaps. And they say things, words of little meaning.

A girl called Sarah Venville is a very strong player. She hits the ball hard, to win. Another girl, called Sarah Cassell, is a graceful player. She hits beautiful shots beautifully, picks the balls up, smiles, laughs, talks, bounces the ball, runs, changes ends ... and all of these things she does beautifully. How can that be?

In Primary School I played sport a lot and was quite good at it, I guess, although the standard wasn't very high. But I even beat the boys at most things. I was an OK hurdler, but that's another story. Well, it's not really. It's all part of the same story. I remember a teacher, Mrs Buckley, telling me I could make the State titles if I took it up seriously, although I thought I had already taken it up seriously. That was in Year Six. I remember my father watching me race on Saturdays. At that stage I was beating the other girls by miles, but he always looked so grim and intense about it that I wasn't sure if I was doing the right thing. Then I crashed over a hurdle that had been left too high after a boys' race and broke my ankle. Somehow it was all different after it mended ... I guess I wasn't as confident and I'd put on too much weight and my father had stopped coming to watch me ... I don't know. It just seemed like everything had changed.

February 11

Today we had classes again.

The weekend is over.

I think I wrote too much in this journal on Friday. All that stuff about the hurdling, and primary school. And my father has found his way into this journal already, when I was so determined that I wasn't going to think about him ever again, much less write about him. It seems he's too powerful still, like a radioactive cloud, finding his dark way into everything. I wonder what it's like where he is? Kind of like here, maybe. Having to line up, always being ordered around, no privacy, no freedom, no flares lighting up the future, showing which way the curves bend, and where are the exits. Perhaps he doesn't talk either ... I mean, I suppose he speaks to people and they speak to him, but it might be just empty, just mechanical words.

Anyway ...

I'm in Prep again. The others seem to be doing so much work. Cathy, the thin one, seems so intense, her serious face absorbed in her work, or something, never looking up. Sophie is the opposite. She's very funny and lively, can't sit still, always getting in trouble because when the teacher comes round to check us she's either talking or out of her seat or something worse. She's pretty, chubby but not fat, looks like a boy a bit;

she has a round face and short hair and red cheeks and a husky voice which makes her sound older when she talks ... like she's twenty-five and sophisticated and sexy.

I wonder what I'd sound like if I talked again now ... like a plastic bottle burning in a fire, I imagine.

February 12

Here is a letter I received in today's mail:

Darling,
Am in a great hurry, so this is just a short note, hoping that you are happy in the new school. J.J. is well and sends his love. We are all very excited about the trip. What would you like us to bring you back? Do you have everything you need for school? I found your flute in the kitchen when I got home, so will send it. Don't give up on your music, darling; you were so good at it.
Love,
Mum.

Am I happy in the new school? No, but perhaps it is better than the hospital in some ways. Not so many weirdos, better food, no more group therapy. In the hospital I felt exposed, under the white light; here I feel like a black snail, crawling around with it on my back, living under it, hiding in it.

There is only one question she really wants answered and that is the question she cannot bring herself to ask:

'Have you started talking yet? Or are you still my daughter, the silent freak?' She's probably found out from the housemistress anyway. I bet she's rung her up to find out if I'm chattering away like a little pet monkey.

I haven't played my flute for nearly a year, since all this started, but she probably hasn't even noticed that. Is music a kind of talking, I wonder?

February 13

Today the English teacher, Mr Lindell, checked our journals. He did not read them, just had us hold them up so he could make sure we were writing in them. I am writing in mine. I am a good girl. A little suck, yuk yuk.

I will write about my Prep desk. It is very plain, brown, with three shelves facing me, for books. One of the shelves is full of textbooks; another one has some writing paper and pens; the third one, the bottom one, is empty.

The other desks are full of decorations and other colourful things. Cathy has lots of books of her own (I mean personal books that she reads for her own pleasure) and a cactus plant that she calls Alberich, and a small toy wombat, and a poem pinned up that I think she wrote herself. And a lot of other things. I like the poem very much. Sophie has mainly posters of pop stars, and pencil sharpeners and stickers and rubbers, all in different shapes and sizes and colours.

In the dorm I have a little cupboard beside my bed, with shampoo, conditioner, deodorant and tissues on it. I use grey school blankets but most of the other beds are covered by doonas that girls have brought from home, with vivid doona covers. My favourite is Ann Maltin's on the bed opposite me. It looks like a jigsaw of stars: white on a dark background. But it is a jigsaw: none of the stars is complete.

I am always first in bed and I often lie there looking at the fragmented stars, trying to put them together. I suppose Ann must have been watching me doing this. Last night she looked across at me and said: 'They do fit together, but it took me years to figure it out.'

I was very embarrassed at being noticed like this and I turned away and buried myself in the pillow. She was being kind, I know; she seems like she's always a kind and gentle person from what I've seen of her so far, but I don't want to be noticed by anyone, for anything.

February 14

Today is Valentine's Day. Most of the girls kind of went mad with it all. Sophie got a card and danced around the dorm at lunchtime, giggling and showing everyone and jumping on all the beds, including mine. I hated her jumping on mine. She can be really over the top sometimes, really hyperactive. Ann got a couple of cards, which didn't surprise me: she's got long hair that's really sandy, like long strands of sand on a beach, and she's pretty and so nice. I think Cathy got a couple too, but she didn't tell anyone. As for me, yes, sure, I got bagfuls, thousands of cards from secret lovers and admirers everywhere ... 'The girl most likely to', that's me.

February 15

They had trials for the school tennis teams yesterday.

I went again — like I said before in here, it's compulsory — but again I just watched from outside the fence. Sarah Venville won all her matches so easily. She's only in Year Nine but I think she could beat most of the Year Twelves. Sophie's hopeless — she misses everything and just won't take it seriously.

I don't mind going, I guess.

Today Mrs Graham, the housemistress, spoke

to me. She said: 'Now we've given you a good long time to settle in and I expect you to start contributing more. I don't want you to opt out. I know you've had a difficult time in the past twelve months and I'm arranging for you to see Mrs Ransome, the school counsellor, twice a week. But we've got a good friendly group of girls in Year Nine and I'm sure, if you make the effort, you'll find them very easy to get on with.'

That's what she said ... more or less.

I don't think I've had a good long time to settle in at all. I mean, I've only just started here. Am I supposed to be grateful that they've taken me, the nut-case, the psycho with the deformed face? They already sponsor a student in the Philippines: some little girl with a lung disease or something. So am I their local project, their domestic act of charity? Mrs Graham walks around looking so perfect, with hair like a puffed-up dried flower arrangement. I don't think she's a very patient kind of woman. And another thing, if the Year Nines are so friendly, I haven't noticed it. I admit some of them tried a bit, in the first few days, but I gave my famous impression of a cockroach and that put them off without much trouble. Yet I can see that some of them are nice, even some of the ones in my dorm.

I wonder if any of them pray? Anyone in this dorm, I mean.

13

February 17

Sophie got angry at me today. She yelled at me quite a lot and shook me by the shoulders. It was because I had not done my job properly in the dorm (we all have jobs: mine was to sweep the staircase) and because of that we failed Inspection and because of that she could not go out on leave till after lunch. So she was angry.

I left the dorm. I heard Cathy say to her: 'You know we're not supposed to yell at her. 'Sophie said something about vegies, vegetables.

I went to the chapel, where we'd had a service only about two hours before. I'd found the service pretty boring but I still went there anyway, and sat there for a long time. It was very quiet, very old. I was inside the stone, where it was cool and peaceful.

I don't know what I thought about, sitting there. Well, I do really, but it's hard to write such stupid stuff down.

I could feel the water inside the stone; hear it, even. Centuries ago — I remember reading this somewhere — churches used to be safe places, where you could hide, and even if the soldiers knew you were there, they had to leave you alone. Something like that anyway. Nowadays it's all changed and there's nowhere safe, except a gaol, and that's the most dangerous place of all. Sitting in the chapel, I remembered the times we had been to church when I was little. Not too many times — Christmas, mostly, and even then my father didn't come very often — but once an old lady took me and after the service she showed me the stained-glass windows, telling me about each one. Sometimes I think about that and wonder if she was my other grandmother, but I doubt it because my mother says I'd have been too young to remember my other grand-parents.

But I remember this lady. She seemed kind.

In this chapel there are six large stained-glass windows and four small ones. My favourite is one of Christ with this girl who's meant to be dead and he's bringing her back to life. Wish someone'd do that to me. The window's got a little plaque under it: 'Sacred to the memory of Sally Aydon, who died after a fall from her horse, January 14, 1937, aged 14. Safe in the arms of God.'

That's the real reason I like the window. Not because I'm religious, 'cos I'm not. But because of this girl, for whom I feel so sad. I thought about her a lot as I sat there in the slow, still chapel. What did her parents do, as the years passed, I wondered? Did they remember her? Did they still mourn? Were they sad forever? Or did it all pass away after a while? I wondered what they did to the horse, too. Could they bear to look at it again?

Anyway, after some time (a few hours I guess) I left the chapel and headed on back to the noise and washing-machine turmoil of it all. When I got back in the dorm a girl called Kate Mandeville was the only one there and she went into a whole big routine: 'Oh, where have you been? Everyone's out looking for you! You missed lunch, you know, but we covered for you, but we were going to have to tell Mrs Graham if you weren't back in another half-hour or so. We thought you were upset about Sophie going off her brain like that. We didn't want her to get in trouble ... or you. Anyway, I'd better go and tell them you're back ...'

So now it's night-time, and I've been sitting at my desk quite a while, writing this. The others are ignoring me a bit — well, they do anyway — but they seem a bit hostile now (or is that my imagination?). There's no Prep tonight, being Sunday, but a few others are at their desks too, catching up on work. I'm going to bed.

February 18

When I read back over the entries in this journal I get an impression of detached confidence. Yet it is not like that at all. Who, upon reading these words, could picture me, slinking along walls, huddled in corners, shrinking from contact, the Year Nine mute, the freak of Warrington? It is not a pretty picture. So the words lie, in a sense, as they always do.

February 19

I make people uncomfortable. The kind ones get angry because their kindness doesn't work. The unkind ones get angry because they think I am attacking them.

February 20

I had my first appointment with the counsellor today. It was forty minutes. She said not to worry about talking or not talking; I could just sit there and use the time any way I wanted. She said that the sessions with her could be just a break from the pressures of school, if that's what I needed most. I don't know what I need. I hoped, after what she said, that it would be peaceful, like being in the chapel, but it wasn't. I kept wondering how much Dr Harvey from the hospital had told her about me.

Tonight Sophie used me as a ventriloquist's doll. She came up behind me as I sat at my desk waiting for Prep to start. She put her hands up the back of my jumper and moved me around as though I were a puppet, speaking for me in a funny voice. Most of the girls laughed, some more than others. Finally a girl called Lisa

Morris told her to stop. I have not mentioned her before, yet in some ways she is the most interesting girl in the dorm, along with Cathy. She is tall and blonde, very Nordic looking, very beautiful, with a slight mark on one cheek (from a skiing accident, I heard her tell someone). I notice that mark every time I look at her. I think she is not a very happy person, yet no-one else is aware of that, because she hides it behind a very strong personality.

After Prep I saw a note on the floor under Anne's desk. Someone had written it to her, I suppose. It said: 'What Sophie did was really off.' Ann had written 'I AGREE' in big letters. There was a lot more, lots of alternating comments, but I moved away because I didn't want to be seen reading their notes. They're always writing to each other during Prep.

Maybe Sophie is still angry because of last Sunday. Even though I was in the wrong then for not doing my job properly, somehow, because I went 'missing' for all that time after she yelled at me, it put her in the wrong with the other girls. It's not really fair, but that seems to be the way it has worked out. Also, I think, from something I heard, that Sophie went out on leave after lunch, like she'd arranged, leaving the others wandering around the school looking for me. It's funny how Sophie's so noisy and I'm completely silent, yet I still can win 'arguments' with her without really doing anything, and even if I'm not in the right.

I'm sitting in bed writing this now, waiting for 'lights out'. A few minutes ago Ann came across to the foot of my bed and said: 'Gee, you really take that journal seriously. What do you write in it all the time?' I just went red, stopped writing and shrank away, until she went back over to her bed. It's not that I want to be so cold and unfriendly ... I just don't know what to say to people, and I can't speak anyway: my throat locks up and my tongue gets all swollen. I don't want them to take any interest in my writing though: I'm scared that some-one might try to read it someday. Anyway, there are other girls who take them more seriously than I do ... Ann writes in hers all the time too, and so does Cathy, and there's a girl called Tracey who has turned hers into a work of art, with wonderful drawings and decorations and beautiful lettering. Sophie's is good too — she sticks all kinds of funny pictures in it, and lots of objects, like movie-tickets and M&Ms and some really way-out things, like a stone that she says she chucked at Mrs Graham's car the other day, and an empty tube of toothpaste. Mine is pretty dull by comparison. Well, *really* dull, actually.

February 21

For English Prep tonight we had to write a poem starting with the line:

> *In the silence of the night*
> *I ...*

I wrote:

> *In the silence of the night*
> *I slept.*

Poems are dangerous.
Cathy wrote:

> *In the silence of the night*
> *I walked across a plain*
> *Of falling flowering snow*
> *And gentle dancing rain.*

There was more, but that was all that I saw. I like her poems. I don't like mine and I don't like the thought of handing it in tomorrow. I won't get in trouble, because they all treat me as 'special' and they don't know whether I should be working or not and they're scared to get mad at me, but it seems rude to write a 'non-poem' like mine when I actually like English and I like the teacher. To hand it in seems to be saying the opposite. I remember in Year Five I had a teacher called Mrs Buchanan. She was a friend of my mother's. One day we had to do what she called 'Creative Writing' and I wrote a whole lot of stuff about a fight that my father and mother had had at home the night before. I was pretty upset about it, I guess, because I remember crying a bit as I wrote it, in the back corner of the room. Anyway, I must have said something too abusive in it (I think I called my mother a selfish bitch) 'cos Mrs Buchanan went off her brain at me and when my mother picked me up that afternoon she gave her my book to read. It was pretty bad. My mother just froze. It was about a week before she would even speak to me again. That was good, in a way, but I was glad when it ended. I don't think she ever told my father though ... I should at least be grateful for that, I guess.

February 22

Had a letter today:

Darling,
I rang Mrs Graham last night. She said that you had settled in well but you weren't making much effort to involve yourself in the life of the House. Darling, I do think that's such a pity. Warrington has given you such a good chance and there are so many opportunities for you at a school like that. I do wish you'd try a few things. Mrs Graham says the Year Nine girls are a particularly nice group this year, and you mustn't cut yourself off from them. I hope we get a more positive report from her next time we ring.

We leave on Monday for New York, so must make this quick and then get on with the packing. We'll be back late March, but you know to contact Grandma if you need anything. We'll send you lots of postcards and bring you back lots of lovely presents.

All my love,

Mum.

P.S. Don't forget Grandma's birthday on March 3. A card would be nice.

A card! Huh! Last time I gave her a card I was about six or seven and I made it myself. Not knowing what to put on it, I went into the newsagent and memorised a message that was on a card in there. I can't remember now exactly what it was, but there was a chicken and an egg and some message about 'your birthday being a good time to get laid'. It didn't make much sense to me but I figured the adults would work it out. They did. That was the last time I made any birthday cards.

February 24

It's a Sunday again. It seems that on Sunday afternoons the dorm separates, splits up, and all its parts go aimlessly off in different directions, tracing out ragged and untidy paths. Then, around sunset, all the parts coalesce.

I like the word 'coalesce'. Though when I look

at it for a long time it seems strange and ugly.

I've been here less than three weeks but it feels like three months. I've been reading back over this journal, fragments of my life here, tears in the curtain. The routines of this school and the personalities of the people seem so familiar already, yet at first they seemed like a game of 'Dungeons and Dragons'. So did the hospital, back in the early days, I guess.

There are eight girls in the dorm: Cathy, the thin, tall writer of poems; boyish, pretty Sophie, who's so bubbly and lively but who finds me so irritating; kind Ann of the spangled doona cover; strong and silent Lisa, who stuck up for me that one time, but so private inside her cold Scandinavian marble mountain. All of these have found their way into this journal already, though that was never my intention. I think, too, I have mentioned Kate, who's loud and kind of crude; her main interests in life are boys and sex, or sex and boys (it depends). She talks about either or both these topics every night after lights out. She reminds me of Edwina at the hospital, who claimed she'd had two abortions already. And then there's Tracey, who's quiet and bland and taken for granted by everyone. She's a bit of a suck; works hard, but I don't think she's very bright, and she's pretty big and sort of ungainly, so that she's not exactly great looking, but she seems kind. Also, there's Emma, who's got red hair and braces and is from Hong Kong, and whom I don't know very well yet, although she talks a lot about all the servants that they've got back in Hong Kong.

And there is me.

I quite like writing in this journal on Sundays 'cos there's no rush, no pressure. Right now it's just before lunch and I'm sitting on the steps that go from the study to the little garden. This morning Cathy and Emma, who have become friendly with each other these last few days, asked me if I wanted to go for a walk down to the beach with them. I didn't go, of course, though it was kind of them to think of me. One day I would like to go there on my own but I cannot go through the processes of asking for and getting permission. (Silence, always my fortress, sometimes my prison.)

Mrs Graham told me that Grandma had rung and sent her love and might be taking me out next weekend.

4 PM:

After lunch I watched all the cars arriving at the boarding house, all the parents taking their daughters out for the afternoon. All the families arriving. I watched from behind a tree, in the garden. How strange it was — so much movement, so many laughter. (I know that's not good grammar but it seems more accurate for what I saw and heard than 'so many laughs' or 'so much laughter'.) The voices sounded a little ... oh, I don't know ... aluminium? But only a little, and some seemed so warm and natural and relaxed with love and happiness. It was a strange scene. I wondered what they talked about all afternoon, these daughters and sisters, with their families. Was it a strain to think of topics of conversation? Were there uncomfortable pauses as people tried to think of things to say? I wanted to call out warnings to them, to sit at the top of a lighthouse in the middle of the lawn and scream desperate warnings: 'DON'T TRUST THEM! LOOK OUT! THEY HATE YOU! THEY HATE EVERYONE! THEY HATE EACH OTHER!' Yet I knew that for a few of them that wasn't necessarily true; they lived in a strange foreign world of love that I envied but could not understand — and would never enter.

When I talked to my parents it was so hard and forced. I was always nervous, and scared of the gaps and the silence. I would try to think of things that I could talk about before I entered a room that I knew they were in.

All that practice made me a regular little star in 'Show'n'tell'. Every hour of my life was a 'Show'n'tell' session.

I tried to imagine what it would be like living in a family like the ones these girls belonged to. It was a jealous dream but a pleasant one, and all the characters and props were provided by the colourful people who were coming and going along the broad gravel driveway.

But then something terrible happened, something that to me seemed terrible. I heard a noise above me, a rustling of leaves and branches. I looked up and saw Lisa Morris (the cold and beautiful Lisa) sitting high above me, hidden in the tree. She had been watching me all that time — and all that time I had been relaxed, at ease, not worrying about controlling my face. And she must have seen all my expressions during the whole time. I am trembling even now, as I write this. To have shown so much! Our eyes met for a moment, while I was still too startled to do anything, and so she was able to see another expression on my face, that of astonishment and horror. But I cannot interpret the way she looked at me. Then I ran away.

I write too much in this journal. But it seems that I cannot help myself. I had trained myself to live without a voice and now I have almost been forced into using one again. What if anyone ever reads this? Mr Lindell says he's just making sure they're not full of swear words and obscene drawings. The other girls say to him: 'You taught in a boys' school too long sir; we're not like that.' But if he could hear Kate talking in the dorm after lights out ... !

Again a session with the counsellor, Mrs Ransome. I don't know how many of these I've had now. They were meant to be every Wednesday and Friday but she keeps changing the times, and, anyway, it seems to be more like three sessions a week instead of two. Does that mean I'm worse than they thought I would be? I'm sure she's a nice lady but I don't do anything in there except sit. Usually she just reads or goes through papers, but sometimes she talks a bit. Today she told me about her son, who's been expelled from his school for smoking dope, and now he goes to a high school. Seems like they have a lot of trouble controlling him. It's bad when the counsellor's kids get into trouble. If they have problems, then I guess everyone will. Erle, at the hospital, was supposed to be a psychiatrist's son, or so people said. I never asked him.

God, I just realised how dumb that last sentence is! As if!

Prep started off in pretty wild fashion tonight. Kate got locked in a wardrobe for the first half-hour and they only let her out a minute before Mrs Graham walked in. There was a Bible in the wardrobe and Kate spent the whole time she was in there yelling readings from it through the door. I don't know what to think when that kind of stuff happens. I can see how it's funny and all, but it makes me very nervous too, as though there are no rules any more, no order, no structure.

Then, at Break, Sophie was leaning back on the window, eating some toast and explaining how she was going to run the school when she was school captain, when suddenly the window shattered and she fell straight through. God, I don't know how she didn't cut her throat on the glass or something. I was frozen into a white silence of utter horror but Sophie was laughing so hard that it seemed like the only real risk she was running was that she would choke on her toast. I guess everyone was just in a crazy mood.

February 26

If I could do that English Prep from last week again, the poem, I'd write this:

In the darkness of the night
I could hear the walls creak
In the corridor
And the doors shuffle past me
One by one
And splashes of dim dusk on the floor.
Pale pools of light that fall apart
As it all grinds shut around me.

That was what the hospital was like, in a way.

Sometimes I think I'm good at English. But everything I write, I end up hating. For instance, now I don't like the last line of the poem. And I should've put something in to explain how there can be 'pools of light' in the darkness of the night. I meant the night lights in the ward. All in all I was in about four different wards in the hospital. But it's the psychiatric one I remember most vividly, 'cos I was in there the longest, of course, but also because it seemed to make the biggest impression; I don't know why. Partly it was the shame of being in there. Partly it was all the weirdos and freaks, like the old lady who wanted all her food heated, even lettuce and ice cream. Partly it was the group therapy too. Of course I never spoke in there — or anywhere — but I listened, I sure listened. I got used to hearing people analyse themselves and other people, and talk pretty openly about themselves, and I suppose after a while I started doing that inside myself. A bit, anyway. Now I do it in this journal — like saying how ashamed I was to be in the psych. ward. I couldn't have said that once. I couldn't even have recognised that thought as being in my head but, hearing other kids talk in group therapy about it, I realised how bad I felt for ending up in such a place — and now I've actually written it down. Dr Harvey would be proud of me.

February 28

I don't want to write anything today.

March 1

Or today. Or today. Or today. Or tomorrow.

March 2

Things aren't exactly good for me here, you know. And nothing seems to help. Including writing it all down. I got accused of stealing on Wednesday. But I didn't do it.

March 4

Grandma came today, this afternoon. We drove into the city and looked in some of the shop windows. Then we went to a movie called *No Love Lost*. It was cute. I liked it. And I didn't really mind being out in public. There weren't many people around. I don't care that much about my face. That's not the problem.

Yesterday was Grandma's birthday. I didn't forget. I thought about it all day. But I couldn't tell her.

March 5

I seem to have spent a lot of time in the chapel the last few days, including last night and this afternoon. If someone else is there when I go in then I leave again. But mostly it's empty. Sometimes, someone'll come in when I'm there, but they usually don't see me, 'cos I sit at the side, in the darkest places. And they're mainly people I don't know anyway. But last night Lisa Morris came in and sat there for about an hour. (At least she's come down from her tree. Maybe she's following me around.) Then, this afternoon, when I first went in, Emma was there. That surprised me 'cos she always seems so cheerful. Maybe cheerful people like to sit in chapels too. Maybe she's religious. Maybe everybody gets down sometimes. I don't know.

I don't even know what draws me to it. I'm not religious.

The library is my other refuge. I often go there at lunchtime and after school. Sometimes I look at books, but mostly not. There's a kind of group of refugees who are there a lot: all the social outcasts of the school, who hide in corners in the library, while the bright and colourful macaws flock to the centre, reading *Mode* and *Vogue* and the boys' school magazines.

I don't read books much, not any more. Oh, I read *The Hobbit* last year, and *Go Ask Alice*, and we did *The Outsiders* and *Thunderwith* in English. This year I just look at the pictures. My all-time favourite book was *The Children of Cherry-Tree Farm*, and I'm not sure why. I like the way all the children in it eat jam and cream and go for rambles (never walks, always rambles) and feed chooks and get tucked in at nights and get treats. And I like Tammy the Wild Man. One thing I don't like though is the way the trains in those books always go *clickey-clack, clickey-clack*. They never go *schroneggy schromk plut*.

Tracey, the dorm suck (no, I shouldn't say that, she can be nice, and she does some wild things) is reading the *Billabong* books again. That seems a bit pathetic, in Year Nine. She takes some rubbishing sometimes but she doesn't seem to mind. Cathy reads cosmic stuff like *Illusions*. I think you can tell a lot about people from what they read. Sophie, for instance, reads Mills and Boons and Sweet Dreams, even though she's embarrassed about it. But the other girls borrow them quite often, so they can't give her too hard a time.

I wonder if they realise how much I notice about them? They probably haven't got a clue, because I never look at them or show the slightest interest. But I'm very aware of everything. I remember seeing an old film once where a father says to his son: 'Son, when your mouth's open, you're not learning anything.' If that's true then I'm well on the way to becoming the world's wisest woman.

March 6

So much doesn't go in this journal and that's frustrating, because then it's incomplete. I can't believe how quickly I've become hooked on keeping it.

Went to tennis practice yet again today. It's still compulsory, even though I haven't touched a racquet or a ball so far this year. I used to be an OK player, I guess. Before I died. (Why did I write that? It was a sudden impulse. 'Cos I'm one of the living dead, that's why. Whatever happened to the happiest days of my life? Afraid of mirrors, afraid of photos, afraid of memories ... afraid of living, that's *moi*.)

Every Saturday, so far, when they've had interschool tennis, I'm listed as one of the reserves. At the *bottom* of the reserves. What a joke. It's just a way to make sure I go. What if all the players and half the reserves suddenly got food poisoning or appendicitis or morning sickness? Would they put a racquet in my hands and push me onto the court? I hate going to these other schools — I imagine everyone's looking at me, and sometimes there's no doubt that they are. At Warrington, though it startles me to realise it, I guess I'm starting to feel mildly safe. That's dangerous — I'd better be careful there.

Today Sophie actually beat one of the other girls (admittedly only a Year Eight, but still . . .). Then she tried to do a victory leap over the net, but it took her four tries and even then she tripped and went flying. She's a real attention-seeker. Or a clown. Or both. Right now in Prep she's throwing grapes at Cathy, across my desk, and Cathy's trying to catch them in her mouth. Emma just told them to shut up 'cos she's scared we'll get in trouble, and besides, everyone's got lots of Prep. But Emma hasn't got a lot of author-ity in this dorm. Lisa's the only one they'd listen to in this situation, and she's ignoring them, working away at her desk. Now Kate's joining in — she's just started chucking peanuts at Sophie. There'll be a food fight in a minute. Part of me wants to join in, part of me's terrified. I guess I sort of smile at it, deep down. God, a year or two ago I would have been running across the desks, pouring milk on everyone's heads. Guess that's what I meant before about living death.

March 7

I am the Phantom, the Ghost Who Walks, in the dorm, in class, all around the school. People don't notice that I exist any more. I like it that way. Sometimes they look at me with sympathy, or say or do something kind, like offering me a bite of a Mars Bar. At those times they use the sort of voice people have when they're talking to little children or pet puppies. Other times they get angry at me and yell. Other times they're cruel and make jokes about me. Mostly it's Sophie, but I don't want to make her sound like she's evil or anything. She just likes people who are loud and funny and noisy. I know it must be awful for them, having me in their dorm. But I did not steal her money. What would I want with money?

Today Cathy got fed-up with me, for no particular reason that I know of. She came into the dorm in a bad mood, swearing at everyone and complaining about everything. Then she found some of my undies on her bed, where I'd put them while I was sorting my laundry. She got mad and threw them at me and said: 'And don't think we're going to keep feeling sorry for you all year.' I was scared and very very sick inside me but I didn't run away like I normally do.

Now we're in Prep again and she has sent me a note:

I'm sorry about yelling at you. I was in a foul after Science, 'cos Hardcastle virtually accused me of cheating. It wasn't anything you did. I'm sorry — I think you're nice and I want to be friends.
Cathy.

It's about 20 minutes since she sent it to me. I cannot look at her. I cannot move. I have spent the whole time with my head down, looking at this page. Now I have just started writing again. I want to die or hide or run away. I am scared to look at her. I can handle, have handled, most things in my life, but not this.

March 8

How strange it is to be liked. I am accustomed to hatred and am more comfortable with it. But I doubt if she meant it. I think she was just feeling guilty about yelling at me.

In group therapy a lot of the talking was about family fights and stuff like that. But their fights did not seem like mine. In my ex-family my mother would yell and scream quite a lot and rush upstairs. But my father just went into a brooding quietness, an ugly silence, that went on forever and scared me forever. (*Scared* me forever, *scarred* me forever; I just realised how alike those two words are.)

Sometimes I wonder if my father said anything at all at his trial; I should have gone perhaps, though, of course, once he'd pleaded guilty I didn't have to go. Did he plead guilty just to protect me from having to stand up in that courtroom and give evidence? Mrs Olsson said that to me once, when she was trying to get me to talk again.

I wonder if he's thinking about me tonight, or any other time? I suppose he probably does sometimes. Funny, that had never occurred to me before. I suppose I'd loom quite large in his life in some ways. I'd never thought about myself as being important to him. They asked me if I hate him and I suppose I do. But the really important thing is to know whether he hates *me* or not. Well, I assume he does ... so what I want to know is, how much? How much does he hate me? A thousand million times over, or just a hundred million times over? And why? What did I ever do to him? I wasn't so bad, was I?

Well ... I guess I was. Guess I must have been. Somehow my relationship with my mother seems unimportant compared with that.

March 9

The other girls swim a lot before school, after school, at weekends. I don't. I'm scared to. Not of the water but of the laughter and splashing and the shapes people's bodies make in the air and when they break the surface of the water. But what I do like is to be at the pool before they come, and to see the way the air and the water are so clear and undisturbed. Then the first girl jumps or dives in — and it all cracks. And the cracks spread quickly and everything shatters. When the pool and the area around it are full of

girls then everything is in a million million fragments, like windscreen glass when it is hit by a
stone. But finally they all go and everything
becomes still and whole again — so quickly that
it amazes me.

I know this is weird and stupid, to think about
stuff like that, but I do.

Mrs Ransome, the counsellor, told me today
that her son wants to leave school and go on a
surfing trip with some older guys. It doesn't
sound like a good idea to me. Mrs Ransome's
pretty worried about him. I like the way she
chats on, some days. She asked me if I'd ever
used any drugs. They all ask me that. I just
looked at the wall, like always. But I haven't, of
course, except when I had to in hospital. I don't
think that counts.

I wonder how many other students go to Mrs
Ransome? Seems like she mainly does careers
advice and stuff like that.

March 10

Tennis today was against St Margaret's, at St
Margaret's. I had to go, God knows why, but I
liked the bus trip, looking through the windows
at the suburbs, and listening to the girls talking.
All the big stars were up the back: people like
Sarah Venville and Sarah Cassell and Lisa
Morris. They sounded like they were having fun.

Cathy hasn't really been any different to me since the note. Well, I don't know. She kind of looks at me more, I guess. I hated myself for not answering the note, but I couldn't. I wanted to, but I couldn't. But today, this afternoon, the dorm was deserted — most people were swimming and Emma's on weekend leave with Tracey. No-one was around — and I did something really dumb. I don't know why, but I went to the garden I really like (the one where Lisa was sitting in the tree that day) and I got a flower and I put it on Cathy's bed. I don't even know what kind of flower it was, for Chrissake! I know it was a really corny thing to do, but that's what I did.

The dorm's been a bit mixed-up lately. Kate and Sophie have terrible fights and yell and scream and throw things at each other, then spend the rest of the day going round to everyone else in Year Nine, trying to convince them that they're in the right and the other one's a real bitch. Emma's pretty friendly with everyone, except I was surprised when she went home with Tracey, because she doesn't seem to have that much to do with her at school. I guess, when you come from overseas, an invitation to someone's place for a weekend would be hard to resist.

Lisa's friendly with everyone too. Like I think I said before, she has a strong personality, but she uses it in a positive way, so that people like her.

Yet there's always that private core that she doesn't let anyone see. I know it's there, from the way she goes off by herself sometimes, but most of the time she seems confident and happy. She's sort of the leader of the dorm in some ways. Kate says some really bitchy things about her behind her back, but I think she's just jealous.

Everyone seems to have ganged up on Ann lately, but not for any reason that I can see. I think she's sweet, and she's always kind to me, but they call her a suck, and backstab her a lot. She had a big fight with Tracey yesterday. Then this morning Sophie went off at Cathy 'cos Cathy used her washing powder without asking, though Sophie's always borrowing everyone else's things without permission. And then Kate stormed out because some of her tapes were missing. She didn't come back for about an hour and missed Inspection and nearly missed the bus for a swimming carnival she was meant to be in.

March 11

I think Cathy must have known the flower was from me, because she didn't say anything, and if she thought it was from anyone else she would have said something. She's got it in a glass of water on her bedside cupboard.

When I read that note again I realised she didn't actually say that she liked me. I think she just meant that she wanted to be friendly, and not mean. I hope I haven't made a fool of myself.

March 12

Emma and Tracey are in trouble for being late back from leave and for being half-drunk too, though the school can't do much about that, seeing it was Tracey's parents who gave it to them. I think they'll be gated. Everyone thinks it's a big joke, Tracey being the *Billabong* girl and all. I don't think she's ever been in trouble for anything like this before. Sophie and Kate, in particular, are killing themselves laughing and giving them heaps. I guess it's pretty ironic, considering that Sophie and Kate have worked their way through at least two bottles of Tequila already this term.

Mrs Graham was so angry though. My insides get washed away by cold waves when teachers get angry like that. I hate it. I want to crawl under the bed and cover myself with blankets in that dark little cave and stay there forever. Instead, I shrink into the wall and huddle there like an idiot.

March 13

Ann had a ceramic piece that she's made herself on the cupboard beside her bed. It was a big bird, an eagle, in shades of brown, and it was very beautiful. She's so artistic. This morning I was vacuuming the dorm, which was my job before Inspection, and I tripped over the vacuum cleaner and fell into the cupboard and knocked the statue to the floor, where it broke into many pieces. It was awful — oh God, it was awful! I write about it so calmly, but inside I was dead, I wanted to die. I went outside; I felt as though all the colour had gone out of my skin, out of my body. I couldn't go back to the dorm. All day I wanted to kill myself; I thought of all the different ways I could kill myself, for the thousandth time in my life. How could I be so clumsy and stupid? And to Ann, who's always been so nice?

I went back in the afternoon, after school, because I had to change. I crept in but Ann and Emma and Tracey were there. Emma and Tracey looked at me, strangely I thought, but I'm used to that. I went along the wall, pressed into it as always, to my corner. Ann came over and touched me on the shoulder and said: 'Don't worry about it — it's nothing. I'm not worrying about it.' I was pressed into the wall as hard as could be, almost going *through* the wall, getting bruises on my shoulder and forehead and knee.

For the second time this term I nearly cried, but I didn't. It was the first time anyone has touched me at this school. My skin felt like a ripe purple plum where she touched me. Emma and Tracey were being busy, deliberately busy, at the other end of the dorm, but it was like they were tuned in, with fine tuning, and all the air was quivering with what was happening.

Tonight Ann already had the eagle glued together again, but I can see the cracks. I will always see them.

March 14

There was a postcard from New York today:

> Darling, hope you're well. We had the worst time with the airline but are finally here. Have hardly seen J.J. — meetings, bloody meetings!
> Love,
> *Mum*.

On the front is the most God-awful picture of some hairy ape climbing the Empire State Building. Maybe it's my so-called stepfather. She thinks it's really cute calling him J.J. — but it gives me indigestion.

Speaking of indigestion, food tonight was these big gross purplish-red frankfurts, with scoops of mashed potato. No-one could eat them but Kate made a pretty creative sculpture out of hers that got even the prefect on duty smiling. It's not often a Year Twelve laughs at a joke that a Year Nine makes. Kate's definitely crude but she's also funny sometimes.

The food's not always bad — in fact on average it's probably better than at the hospital. One thing I can't get used to though is the amount of noise in the dining room. At the hospital, in the psych. ward anyway, there was never much noise in the dining room. People used to just sit there looking glum. The best night was when they found that an old guy called Frank, who had just come in, had put all his dinner in his pocket and was eating it out of there with a spoon. There was pandemonium that night — the staff went bonkers. I think it was only the patients who could see the funny side.

I wonder if my father will ever write to me? I wonder if he's allowed to write letters? When I turned twelve he was away on a business trip somewhere and he sent me a birthday card. That's the only time I've had mail from him, I think. I'd hardly recognise his handwriting if he did write. I wonder what he'd say? 'Um, sorry.' Doubt it.

What makes me sick is all these American TV shows where everyone gets on so well together, and the parents are so understanding and caring and compassionate and everyone always talks over a problem and that way they solve it. I hate

it. God, when I think I used to cry over programmes like that!

March 15

I know I haven't said much in this journal about
the school subjects ... mostly because they seem
to matter so little. Yet I care about them and I
want to do well. I listen in class quite a bit and
try to understand, but I don't write a lot in case
the teachers notice me. Mrs Graham has me for
Maths and I'm too scared of her to do much. I
like History, with Dr Thorley. The worst one is
P.E., even though they don't make me do anything. But watching everyone else makes me feel
so out of it.

We have Dr Whiteley, the Headmistress, for
Divinity. I like to sit and look at her as she talks,
and to listen to her. She seems so perfect, always
so well-dressed and well-groomed, never anything out of place. I remember, at the interview
with her, thinking that we might be on a TV set,
because she looks like the lady who introduces
the opera on television. Quite often she doesn't
turn up for Divinity and I'm always disappointed
a little (although we get enough religion here to
last a lifetime).

But English is the best. It's the only subject I do
much writing in, but that's mainly in this journal
and I go to a lot of trouble to make sure no-one

can read it. Mr Lindell's English classes are meant to make you think, I guess, about yourself and people and everything. Some of the kids say it's pretty weird, but they're more honest in English than they are anywhere else, and they say more about what they feel.

Yesterday we had to draw an abstract self-portrait, a kind of symbolic thing, then explain it to the rest of the class. It's amazing what people said. Lisa Morris drew a whole lot of pale pastel colours but they were split in half with a vivid jagged gash, like a bolt of lightning. She wouldn't talk about it though. Cathy drew a person — herself — being forced along a kind of tunnel by a lot of grey shapes. She said they were like her teachers and parents and stuff. 'And other students?' Mr Lindell asked. Cathy said 'Yes' to that. But the fascinating thing for me was the number of people, like Cathy, who drew things showing them on their own and with various pressures on them, feeling isolated, with the group against them. I wonder if they know what isolation means? Perhaps they do.

Mr Lindell quoted something he'd read: 'We're all so curiously alone, but it's important to keep making signals through the glass.' What signals do I make? None at all, unless everything I've done in the last eleven months has been a signal. But there's so much glass. Very thick — but no matter how thick it is, it's still transparent.

Having me in the class inhibits everything though. People were talking quite openly about the things they do to make friends and keep friends; then a girl called Sandy Bennett started saying how awful it would be not to have any friends, and in a moment a cool pink breeze blew through the room and embarrassment brushed every face. They've become so used to me that normally they forget I'm there, but then something like that happens and they remember. Yet I was so fascinated by what they were saying that I wanted them to go on forever.

Everything that's said in English etches itself clearly and sharply in my mind, like letters carved neatly into deep frost. But I never let them see how eagerly I listen.

March 16

A week today is the Easter break. I'm going to my grandmother's, as Mrs Graham informed me today. My 'parents' (as she called them) won't be back from America till after Easter. Then Mrs Ransome told me that I've got an appointment with Dr Harvey on the Tuesday. So that's Easter taken care of.

Mrs Ransome said her son has settled down a bit lately — he gave up the surfing trip idea and he's still at school. That's nice for her.

The dorm's been pretty awful today. Ann's not

well and has been in sick bay for two days, although they all say she's faking. They're horrible about her when she's not here — but she's more popular again now than she was a few weeks ago. Probably Tracey's the one they're nastiest to at the moment. It seems to be someone different every week, like everyone takes it in turns. But it's really only Sophie and Kate. Everyone else just goes along with them because they're scared of them. Except Lisa — even Sophie and Kate are scared of her, though she's popular as well.

Every time I go in the drying room someone's smoking. Every time I go in the bathroom someone's smoking, or even drinking. Every time I go in the Prep room people are having 'private conversations' and they wait for me to leave, though you'd think they'd hardly bother. Every time I go in the common room they're watching TV, and that's usually what I end up doing. I still go to the chapel or the library sometimes, but not as often as before. But I miss those old friends, those warm silent buildings.

March 17

St Patrick's Day, whatever that proves. The Art teacher, Mr Ross, who's really tiny, came to school all dressed in green and said he was an

Irish leprechaun. I smiled to myself. It reminded me of books that I used to read.

March 18

Last night Ann came out of sick bay. She'd had flu. It was good to see her.

I've realised again how little I say about what I really think and feel in this journal. I mean, I skate the surface but it's too painful to go deeper. Yet I want to. For instance, with Ann, it was *really* good to see her — I felt a rush of blood fill me with pleasure, and if I could have smiled I would have.

But a lot of the time I can't write such things because I don't even know what I think or feel. It's like I'm numb inside. Some of the questions Mr Lindell asks in English I take away and worry about for days and still can't answer. It's like there are no answers.

After lights out last night everyone was talking about their families and stuff. Out of eight people in the dorm, only two, Tracey and Cathy, seem to get on well with their parents. Well, Ann might if they were both alive, but her father died when she was two. Sophie's always talking about how much she hates her mother; Kate hates both her parents and tells amazing stories about the things she says to them and the way they all yell at each other; plus she's adopted, so I guess that hasn't worked out too well. Emma's parents are divorced; then last night Lisa started talking about how her parents are divorced too, since last year. I don't think too many people knew that. That's three out of eight in the one dorm that are split! Three out of eight! I mean, it makes you wonder why kids get sent to boarding school.

Lisa's voice was so low and so quiet when she was talking and everyone was kind of hushed. But they kept asking her questions, like they really cared, and she told them how her parents had fought for so long; then they'd sent her away to Warrington last year and as soon as she got here they wrote her a note to say they were splitting up. She'd been here five days when she got the letter. They told her that they thought it'd be better to put her into boarding school and then tell her, so she'd be in a different environment, or something. Like they were doing her a favour. I'll never forget the way she told it, the sound of her voice in the darkness. Oh, I was tense, listening to it all, so tense there in my bed. My fists were so tight the nails cut into my palms and this morning I found little dried-up blood marks on my hands. But I was sort of pleased about that — I'm not sure why. I wanted to suffer, to feel the pain with her. It was like listening to my own voice in the dark.

March 19

Here is a collection of trivial detail for this journal. Last night's movie was *My Fair Lady*. This afternoon Sophie got caught smoking and now has three hours detention. In chapel this morning Ann kind of passed out — like, fainted — and had to be taken outside. This afternoon everyone in the dorm was out on leave, except Lisa and me. The drive was jammed solid with BMWs and Mercs. And everyone brought masses of food back with them, which they pigged out on tonight. I heard Kate arguing with her parents because Mrs Graham had just told them that Kate wasn't doing any work. Kate wasn't as rude to her parents as she always claimed she was, but she sure was pretty rude. Then she got in a foul mood after tea because one of her posters had been torn and no-one would own up to it.

I watched all the people come and go this afternoon again, hiding in the same garden. Lisa was up her tree once more, but this time I knew she was there. At one stage I looked up at her and our eyes met for a moment. She looked at me gravely, but in a friendly way, before I turned away again. It was nice to know she was there, somehow, yet I thought it was strange, because she could have gone out with anyone she'd wanted, yet she preferred to sit in a tree.

Everybody's pretty excited about going home for Easter, but not me I guess. Everyone else gets to go at lunchtime, but Sophie has to do her smoking detention that afternoon, so she can't go till five o'clock, so she's not too happy.

In English today we had to write answers to a whole lot of questions, like: 'What's a dream you'd like to have?' Most people put funny things, like dreams about film stars, but some were really good. Another one was: 'What's a scene you'd like to see painted?' There were more film star answers that time too, some of them pretty rude. One girl, who's a bit up herself, said: 'Me winning my showjumping event at the State Titles last year.' Another girl, Rikki Martin, a day-girl, who's really intelligent and nice, said 'Infinity'. And someone else said 'God'. Lisa said she'd like a painting of the farm they used to own, which her parents sold when they got divorced and moved to the city. I guess she must miss it a lot. Cathy wouldn't read hers out, which was a shame, because I always listen especially for her answers. I didn't write anything, but I thought, and I'm still thinking. In some ways, in some strange terrible way that I don't understand, I'd like a series of paintings showing every moment of that day when it all happened, nearly a year ago. Even more than the happy days before then.

Happy! That's a joke.

Another question was: 'What are some things people do that make you feel insecure? Secure?' Man, I tell you, these questions hurt my head. The answer to the first one is 'I don't know'; the answer to the second one is 'Nothing'. But both these answers are untrue.

Some of the questions were just funny, light-hearted ones, like: 'If the world's energy crisis worsened to the point that you were only allowed one electrical appliance, what would it be?' Most people put either their tape players, or stuff to do with cooking. Sophie put her hairdryer. I think, for me, it'd be a light.

March 21

We have special Easter services every day this week. I often wonder during chapel how much of it is true.

I'm tired tonight and sick of writing in this thing.

March 22

A hard thing has happened, a terrible thing, and I feel so bad that I couldn't do anything. This afternoon I went to the dorm instead of to tennis practice, like I've done a few times lately (no-one ever says anything about it). Normally I'd have the place to myself for an hour or so at this time, because everyone's at Sport. But today, as I was sitting on my bed eating a candy bar, Lisa came in, went to her bed and lay on it face down. And after a few moments she began crying! I could hear her. And I could see her shoulders shuddering. Lisa, the strong one, who never cries! It got worse: her crying became louder, uncontrolled, sobbing. From deep, deep down. It agitated me so much. It took me a lot of discipline to acquire the total control that I now have but I thought Lisa had it too ... and to see her lose it, realise again how totally on my own I am, was too bad.

I fluttered around the dorm wanting to help her, wanting to do something, say something, to touch her and comfort her. Imagine! Me of all people! I felt like a kind of club-footed moth. I don't even know if she knew I was there.

It's like the hunchback of Notre Dame wanting to help Esmeralda, I guess.

Several times I went close to her, almost close enough to touch, but each time, frightened, I slid away again.

People have cried in the dorm before, of course, many times. But never when I was there on my own. And never such violent crying. And never Lisa.

Eventually, after quite a long time, maybe twenty minutes or so, she stopped. Then she just lay there quietly until people could be heard coming back to the dorm. Then she got up and went into the bathroom to wash her face. When she came out she was laughing and joking with everyone and I guess only I could see what an act it was. That is her mask, I guess, just as mine is silence.

That's all that happened. It mightn't seem much, and I still don't know what she was crying about, but it seems a lot to me.

March 28

Back from Easter tonight. I'm writing this at my desk, just before lights out. I only got in at 8 o'clock and there's been no time. Cathy's not coming back till tomorrow 'cos she's got an orthodontist appointment, but everyone else is here.

March 29

Well, that was Easter, all over now. It's nice to get back to my journal. I hid it on the ledge under my desk while I was away, and covered it with lots of paper and stuff.

Yesterday I saw Dr Harvey at the hospital. It was strange going back there. More than strange, it was scary. I got short of breath and felt sick in my stomach.

And going there as an outpatient felt weird too. I had to go to the office, where kind Mrs Shelby recognised me straight away and asked me how I was going and said nice things. Then I had to sit in the waiting room with the other outpatients, while the inpatients wandered past or came in and out to ask Mrs Shelby stuff, as though they belonged there and were confident and at home. Now I was on the other side, on the outside looking in. I saw none of the people I had really liked, like Erle or Jenny or Brian or Jim, but I did see a few that I recognised — a nice old man who I think was there for alcoholism, and Mrs Farrugia, who had agoraphobia — she recognised me and waved and called out 'Hello'. That made me feel better, as though I was special, not just an anonymous outpatient. And I saw a boy called Noel Harrington, who was one of the school phobia kids, but who'd never taken any notice of me while I was there and obviously wasn't going to start now. I was surprised to see him still there though because the kids with school phobia normally don't stay that long. He must have been worse than I thought.

Anyway, I saw Dr Harvey, and he sent me over to a plastic surgeon, who examined me and said he'd write to my mother, but there wasn't any major work that could be done for a few years yet. I was glad in a way. I didn't think I'd like my face being touched by him but it turned out OK Doctors' hands are so cool and sort of . . . detached.

March 30

Kate talks about her wild Easter and how she was drunk half the time and how she ran away for two days of it, and how she fought with her parents all the way through. Sophie stayed with them for the last two days — they've got a property in the northwest of the state somewhere — and she said the arguments were terrible.

Emma stayed with Rikki Martin because it was too far to go home to Hong Kong just for five days. The others haven't said much, except about the movies they saw and the tapes they bought. Cathy lives on a country property too; Ann lives right in the middle of the city; Lisa I'm not sure about, but I think she lives somewhere in the eastern suburbs.

It's funny how you can be with people for so long and not know much about them. I mean, I guess I know a fair bit about them, as people, but I don't know much about their extended lives, beyond this dormitory. They have parents, brothers, sisters, friends and relatives; in the holidays they go to parties, or they go surfing or skiing; but all that stuff seems quite remote from our lives in here.

Today Mr Lindell was wearing one of those string ties, like the sheriffs in the old movies. It looked pretty funny. He was born in Canada; he talks a lot about the wheatfields and stuff — around Edmonton I think it's called. He's a big man, with fairish, almost gingery hair — he looks like a big bear, and strangely enough his glasses make him look even more like one. A gentle bear though — he has a soft, kind voice. Actually I just figured out who he reminds me of slightly (this is *really* corny now) — the Professor who marries Jo in *Good Wives*. Bet I'm the only one at Warrington who's read that book.

March 31

Easter with my grandmother sure was dull. I was about to say that it was 'quiet' but guess that'd be a bit unfair, seeing that I didn't make a lot of noise. She's nervous of me, I think. I don't blame her for that — I'm nervous of myself! When she collected me she looked like she wanted to hug me, or something, but she held off. I'm glad she did — I'm not exactly into physical contact. Most of the time she just watched TV or fussed around the house. She's got very definite routines with television: certain programmes she *has* to watch, and the whole day is constructed around those. It's mainly the news, quiz shows, stuff like that — plus anything to do with classical music. She really flipped on Saturday night when the ballet was on. To do her justice, she did ask me if I wanted to go anywhere — but I didn't, although I walked through the park opposite her apartment early one morning, when there was a good chance no-one would be around. That didn't work out too well though — I'd forgotten about all the joggers and dog-walkers and council workers and guys like that.

Sunday night she went over to some other old lady's place, but I didn't go. That was the best night really — to be on my own again, when there are so few chances for that at school (and none at all at the hospital). Yet, strangely enough, now I get depressed when I'm on my own. That never used to happen.

We had turkey and stuff for dinner on Easter Sunday, but it seemed pretty stupid when there were only two of us. And I got a big Easter egg. But all I could think about through the dinner was my father: I kept wondering what he'd be eating. As if I should care, after all he's done — and what he's done to me.

My grandmother tried to show me another postcard from my mother in New York but I refused to read it. Grandma didn't press the point. She's not a bad old bag really — she tries and she means well but she doesn't cope too well with things she doesn't understand, and she doesn't really communicate. Guess that must run in the family.

In Art today Mr Ross was talking about how some people think that the greater the suffering the greater the art. God, there ought to be some pretty hot artists in our family then. He said: 'If you had the choice between being a suffering genius and a happy gardener, which one would you be?' For me that's not a choice, although I can't imagine being a happy gardener — I can't stand gardening.

The song everybody keeps playing and singing around here is called 'Fragments':

Fragments of my life were falling
All around, as you sat talking,
Not seeing me with your eyes,
Not hearing your own lies,
Not knowing what you're doing,
To me.

Tomorrow is April Fools' Day. It makes me very nervous. Everyone's full of talk and ideas and jokes. I hate it all and wish it had never been invented.

April 1

April Fools' Day is as good as finished with. It wasn't as bad as it might have been, but I'm glad it's over. People did stupid stuff like putting water bombs on the top of doors and tying socks together and hiding people's shoes. I hate all that garbage. It scares me. It's like there are no rules any more, it's all a big mess, with everyone going crazy. I think they were going to do something to me, because when I was in the bathroom I heard Sophie say: 'Go on, do it,' and Emma said: 'No don't, she might freak out and you'd be in trouble with Graham.' Sophie said: 'She's part of the dorm isn't she?' Then Lisa said: 'Don't. Leave her alone; she trusts us, don't mess it up.' They kept talking, I'm pretty sure, but their voices dropped from argument volume to conversation volume.

I was hoping Lisa had won and I was nervous for a while after I came out of the bathroom, but it seems like they hadn't done anything. I was pleased about what Lisa had said though, and I've been thinking about it all day. I suppose I do trust them a bit (Cathy and Lisa and Ann and Emma anyway), yet when I came to this place I was so determined never to trust anyone, not to let them get to me, not to get involved with anyone, to be cold and stay cold. I've succeeded, I guess, but sometimes maybe to succeed is to fail.

What I can't figure is, how can Lisa say I trust them — that's if it was me they were talking about? I don't give any clues. How can she say that? Maybe she's noticed something that I haven't.

April 2

Last night's film was *Raiders of the Lost Ark*. I hadn't seen it before; I guess I was the only one who hadn't. Quite early in the movie a man grabs a red hot emblem, not knowing it is hot, and the design of the emblem is burnt into his hand ... How hard it is to write these words ... I ran out of the hall across to the garden and hid behind a tree. It was horrible. I hoped no-one had seen me leave. I hate making scenes. But Cathy came after me and put her arms round me and held me. I shook and fluttered and shook. She was crying! I felt with amazement the salt tears on her cheeks in the darkness. I broke free and ran away, back to the dorm, and hid in the bathroom, where the lights were safely out. No-one came, and after a while I went to bed. But I still remember the sight of his hands smoking and burning, and the sound it made, and worse than anything, I could smell his skin burning; there in the hall I could smell it. Now, today, I am still frightened and I still shake when I remember, but worse than anything I feel stupid and embarrassed that Cathy saw me like that.

April 3

I hope you're feeling better. It was so hopeless of them to show that film. I can't believe them sometimes.

When you came here they told us to leave you alone and not to put any pressure on you. Is that what you want? I guess it is. Or is it? We're pretty friendly really but I don't want to upset you. I'm sorry this note's so dumb but I don't know what to write to you. I wonder what you think of us?

Cathy.

Well, that's the note I got last night. She's persistent. But I like her. And I feel a kind of yearning to get to know her sometimes.

Mrs Ransome, the counsellor, had heard about me running out of the movie too. So I guess I made more noise than I realised, getting out of there. She talked a bit about it but mostly today's session was a quiet one, with me sitting there and her doing some knitting. Actually she spent most of the time trying to untangle some wool that she said her little daughter had been playing with. It was a big mess. I got impatient watching her do it — she seemed clumsy and I thought I could have done it in half the time.

April 4

They came back today from New York. Mrs Graham told me they'd rung up. I don't know when they'll see me. I think I preferred it when they were in the US.

April 5

Not good, not good, things are not good.

April 6

Chalk white, chalk white, the colours of the walls in my chalk garden.

April 7

In my waking dreams it all falls apart. In my sleeping dreams there is no 'it' and so no 'apart'.

April 11

I wonder if I talk in my sleep?

April 13

I dreamt last night that I was on a kind of hill, a little dark knoll, and some people, I'm not sure who, brought me a huge white sea monster they had found, all dredged up for drowned, so wet and bloated and dead. Yet gradually, as I touched it, it came to life and thinned down and colour and warmth and life came to its own body. Then we went for a walk and after a while we came to a lake, which it slipped into and, sort of saying goodbye to me, swam away. I was sorry to see it go, yet I knew it was right that it should, so it could be alive and independent.

April 14

I am back in the dorm tonight, having been in sick bay for the last few days. I'm not sure why. But now I'm back here for the weekend and 'We'll see how you feel on Monday, whether you're ready for classes again'.

April 15

While I was in sick bay I heard the Matron talking to one of the teachers — Mrs Pearce, I think — in the dispensary. She said: 'They shouldn't have taken her in the first place unless they were going to do something to help her.' And Mrs Pearce-I-think said: 'She sees Helen Ransome just about every day.' And Matron said: 'Well I can't imagine Helen ever doing much to help anyone. Do you think she's getting any better?' And Mrs Pearce-I-think said: 'Yes, maybe. She moves around the school more confidently. And she looks more relaxed. You've got to expect setbacks like this from time to time. I gather the idea was to take her out of the hospital, where she was making no progress, and put her in an environment with normal kids, to see if that would help.' And Matron said: 'Well, fancy putting her in a dorm with Sophie Smith and Kate Mandeville then!'

I was shocked. I didn't think adults talked about teachers and students like that.

April 16

Cathy brought this journal over to the sick bay while I was in there. Oh God, I hope she didn't read anything in it. I hope, I hope, I hope, I hope, I hope, I hope, I hope.

April 17

Went to classes today. It was OK. We had Art. I splattered little drops of paint all over my sheet of paper by flicking my brush, all different colours. I liked it. When I half-shut my eyes and peered at it, it all came together in a kind of ... a kind of *world*.

I haven't been in too good shape just lately, and so I haven't been using this book much. I hate that. It's like once I start something I've got to keep it going all the way through — and I've got to make it perfect as well. Perhaps I should never have started it — but it's been good for me and I guess I needed something.

I really crashed a week or so ago — that's why I've been in the sick bay. I don't know why that was either.

I can't describe the feeling when I go down — it's down down down and there's never going to be an up again. And whatever was good isn't good any more; white becomes grey, music becomes dictionaries, honey becomes beer and the sky a curdled lemon. There's no caramel any more.

Why does this happen to me and not to other people? Why does this happen to anyone? I can think of things that might have triggered it off. Sure, lots of things: the *Raiders* movie; my mother and stepfather being in the same country as me; a comment I heard a Year Seven make about my face (that I'm not going to put down in here for any money); being scared of Sophie and how cruel she is to me sometimes; getting that note from Cathy; worrying about my father and why I haven't heard from him. (What am I talking about? I don't think I even *want* to hear from him. Do I?)

I realised as I lay there in the sick bay what the worst torture in the world would be, the worst worst suffering that anyone could ever be called upon to endure: it would be to have to sit in a chair and listen to people saying nice things to you, to have to listen to them paying you compliments and being kind and friendly to you. That would be the worst thing. Luckily, it's not likely to happen to me ... ever.

We did a poem in English today though that I liked:

If ever any beauty I did see,
Which I desir'd, and got, t'was but a dreame
   of thee.

I wonder what she felt, having poems like that written about her? Maybe she enjoyed it. It was a nice lesson, in a class where I feel more at ease than I do anywhere else, I think, with a teacher whom I trust. Even Sophie likes Mr Lindell.

April 18

Lisa's reorganised the dorm, so that we share the jobs more fairly and change them round more often. It's better, but I think Sophie gets annoyed at her for taking charge all the time. (Tonight I will write just trivia like that.) Emma was meant to get the supper, and forgot, so we have no supper. For History, we're meant to read two chapters of the textbook and answer the questions, so it's quiet in Prep for once, with Sophie, who's normally the noisiest, telling everyone else to shut up. Tonight Cathy got a phone call that made her cry. I don't know what it was all about, but she was talking to Lisa and Lisa was kind of comforting her, so that was good. Tonight's meal was some kind of black-coloured soup that tasted like furniture polish; then chops with mashed potato and broccoli. And what makes it worse is the way it's cooked. Normally everyone stocks up at the tuckshop to keep themselves alive, but the tuckshop's closed this week because the school's been getting too untidy, with papers and stuff.

Ann was playing a song before Prep started, called 'Legends of Lost Youth'. I wonder if it was about me? It's funny how every song is in a way. She's in the dorm now, practising her violin. She plays it so well. Mrs Ransome told me today that I should learn a musical instrument. She doesn't know I used to learn flute. How strange it would be now — like speaking without a voice. Is that what music is then, a ventriloquist with his doll?

Tracey's got her first period at last, years after everyone else. Well, months anyway. Emma turned it into a big joke, about her being a woman now and everything, and presented her with a rolled up towel that she said would be better for her than a tampon. It was pretty funny, but Tracey'd kill me if she knew I was writing about it in my journal.

I wonder what the others write about? Cathy's been writing pages and pages every night. Some people, like Kate, hardly ever open theirs. Some people show them to everyone and swap them around.

There are times when I think Tracey is more cruel to me than anyone else in the dorm. There can be a malice in the stuff that she does that even Sophie doesn't seem to have. Maybe it's because, next to me, she's at the bottom of the pecking order, so I'm the only one she can take it out on.

Kate's in a foul mood tonight because she's lost a necklace she really likes. One of the toilets is blocked and no matter how many times it's reported they still don't fix it. Mrs Graham backed her car into a delivery truck this afternoon, then gave a detention to some Year Eights who were watching, because they laughed. Sarah Venville, who's just about the best tennis player in the school, got beaten 6–2, 6–2 by Sarah Cassell today.

Yes, like I said, it's all trivia. But I guess at least I am writing a lot in my journal again.

April 19

I hate Science because every time Hardcastle mentions the word 'acid' there's a kind of tension comes into the room. A few people look at me out of the side of their faces, most people look very deliberately in the opposite direction, and even Hardcastle seems embarrassed. I don't mind the word but I mind the way people react and I don't know what I'd do if we ever had to use any in an experiment.

In English today we (although I didn't do it) had to write down an emotion or feeling that we hadn't shared with the class before, then all of them were put (anonymously) into a pile in the middle of the room and they were read out and people talked about them, though we only got through about eight. I must admit to gradually being drawn in by what Mr Lindell was reading and what they were saying. I was so surprised — most of them were about loneliness; people saying how lonely they feel at school sometimes. I didn't think they'd know about anything like that. Well, most of them, anyway. Two of them said they were sick of the backstabbing and arguing that goes on, and one said she was scared of crowds. I looked at all their faces, wondering who that was. But there was no reading those skilful masks, no guessing what was going on underneath their smiles. Yet, like I said before, it's good the way people are quite honest in English.

April 20

Last night the conversation in the dorm went on till after midnight and tonight I'm so tired. They were all talking about the boys they like, which is a common topic of conversation around here.

A girl Sophie knows from home gave her the name and address of some friend who's in prison, a really wild guy. For a joke, Sophie and Kate wrote a letter to him and now he's written back, saying he'll come to visit them when he gets out in a couple of months! They're so stupid! Now they're really scared. Lisa told them to go and tell Mrs Graham but they're not too keen on that idea. I don't know how they're going to get out of it. I blot their fear up too: it soaks slowly into me. I imagine the man's shadow across our ceiling after lights out. I wonder what kind of men my father is having to spend his life with: what kind of man he is turning into.

Lisa likes a boy named Peter Fallon-White, whom she met at the beach, but I think it's a relationship she just has for the sake of appearances. Like going through the motions. Ann says she likes someone but won't say who it is: maybe she's just saying it. Cathy's going with a boy she met at a dance before Easter. I don't think Tracey's going with anyone. Emma's rapt in a boy named Sam Nucifora, who goes to St Patrick's; he writes her passionate letters and calls her up all the time.

As for me, it'd be a strange boy who'd be interested. And I would be scared to have anything to do with a boy. But sometimes I dream, only in the dreams it's not really me anyway. It's too complicated. Sex is so complicated. I wish no-one had ever invented it in the first place. What a mess it's made of everything — like my mother's life for instance. It's dark and threatening and yet it's powerful and draws people towards it. Even me, after everything — it still simmers away inside me.

April 21

Today Mr Lindell came up alongside me as I walked along the corridor towards the dining room. I was close to the wall, as usual, but he walked with me. He said: 'My wife and I are very keen to have you come stay with us for the weekend. We'd like you to come but of course it's up to you. If you want to, then wait out the front after sport tomorrow morning, and I'll pick you up, and bring you back Sunday afternoon. I've cleared it with Mrs Graham, so it's OK with her.'

That was all! He just touched me on the head, then went off towards the staff room, leaving me standing there. I didn't know what to do. I don't know what to do. I want to go but I'm scared to, 'cos I don't know what they'll expect of me. I've seen his wife a few times and I know he's got some little kids 'cos he's mentioned them in class. It's too scary. I don't think I'll go.

April 23

Well, despite what I wrote on Friday night, I went anyway! And I had a good time! Yes, I enjoyed it. I feel a bit strange writing that but I'm still a bit high I guess, having just got back a few minutes ago. It was good! And they're so nice! Nice, nice, nice! How can people be so nice? Mrs Lindell is very lively and very intelligent and very funny. She speaks about six languages. And I don't speak any — not even English! They have two little boys, Stuart, who's seven, and Scott, who's five, and a little girl called Anna, who's three, and so sweet.

On the way there Mr Lindell told me all about them and what to expect. But despite that I got very shy when we got there and the children were kind of crowding round and jumping all over me. I guess they were excited to have a visitor. They wanted to know where I'd be sleeping, and whether I was in 'Daddy's' class, and what it was like being a boarder, and lots of other things. Mrs Lindell pulled them off and calmed them down. She told them that I didn't like to talk; when they asked 'Why?' she said 'She just doesn't like to,' and they got the message not to ask any more.

During the afternoon everyone was outside playing a game that was a mixture of cricket and softball, with a fairly big ball, and several times when the ball came towards me I picked it up and threw it back to them. Not much, hey? But for me a lot.

Then I went in the kitchen, when Mr Lindell started preparing dinner. That surprised me — him doing that! He gave me some vegetables to chop and I did that too. The meal was so good. I kept wondering: is this the way they normally eat, or have they gone to all this trouble just for me? We had home-made carrot and mint soup, then veal and mushrooms and a whole lot of vegetables, then Black Forest torte that Mrs Lindell had made, with ice cream. It was the best meal I'd had for a long time. (My grandmother cooks quite well I guess, but it's always plain. My mother just messes round: besides, they eat out a lot.)

The thing that amazed me most was how nice Mr and Mrs Lindell were with their children. It was really touching. I guess I was unlucky: I think I scored the wrong family.

After tea — this part is hard to put down on paper: I'm trembling a little as I write it — we were watching TV when the little girl Anna came and sat on my lap and cuddled up to me. I didn't know what to do, I got such a surprise, but after a minute I put my arms around her and held her. She was looking up at me — I guess she was sleepy — then, after a minute, she put her hand up to my face and touched my cheek with her finger and said: 'Hurt face, hurt face.' I know I went very red and hung my head, but something in the way she said it seemed to break something inside me and I realised that I was going to cry, and there was no power on earth that could stop it, and even though I fought and fought to hold it back, tears ran down my face and, even worse, some sobbing noises came out — the strange sound of my voice, that I had not heard for over a year. And so I sat there crying and crying and struggling all the time to control it, and the tears ran onto Anna's skin and she started saying: 'She's crying, Mummy, she's crying.' After a while Mr Lindell gently lifted her off me and Mrs Lindell put her arm around me. That just made me more embarrassed, which was good in a way because it gave me the self-control to stop.

Anna said to her father: 'Why's she crying, Daddy?' and he said: 'Because she's not very happy, darling.' Then Stuart and Scott both came and stood beside me and touched me and that nearly started me off again. They're such a kind and loving family — I can hardly believe it.

I went to bed at the same time as the kids, because I was too shy to be around after that. It was a really pretty bedroom but I lay awake for a long time, thinking about everything, especially the crying. I hadn't known if I could still cry. I thought maybe my tear ducts had been damaged. It seemed like I lay there forever, with such a confusion, a huge jumble of thoughts in my head, wondering if it would ever make sense, like looking at the Milky Way and wishing I were an astronomer.

This morning everyone stayed in bed late and the kids were in their pyjamas till nearly lunchtime. It was very informal. Anna brought me in all her dolls and teddies and stuffed toys and told me about each one. She didn't seem to mind that I didn't say anything: she just prattled on for ages. It was nice. Because there was no-one else there, I didn't shrink away or make myself small like I normally would. Anna seemed to trust me so much. I wish, I wish I had a sister.

I was meant to come back to school this afternoon but the Lindells said they were enjoying having me so much they wanted me to stay for tea, so Mr Lindell rang Mrs Graham and arranged it. I think they were just doing it to be kind but I was glad because I wasn't looking forward to coming back to all the bitchiness and fighting in the dorm. But here I am now and used to it again. Mr Lindell drove me back. When I left, Mrs Lindell gave me a hug and so did all the children, especially Anna. Mrs Lindell said: 'They really like you.'

When I came back into the dorm, Sophie was in the middle of a big screaming match with Kate; Cathy was lying on her bed looking depressed and Ann was complaining non-stop about a detention she was given for talking in the chapel. As I write this I can still hear her. 'How do they know I wasn't talking to God?' she asked just then.

April 24

I've recovered from the weekend, I guess, but I'm still confused and mixed-up about it all — about giving way and crying, I mean. I didn't want to do that but I guess it's probably a good thing. Dr Harvey'd certainly think so anyway.

School lessons seem so boring at the moment. In History we're doing Mediaeval History, which I quite like. English is *Lord of the Flies*, which I hate. It reminds me of life in our dorm sometimes. In Maths it's surds — yuk — although it's satisfying when you work them out. Science is all Astronomy and stuff, which I don't get too excited about. I miss my flute sometimes, although I used to get really bored with it when I did play it. But I will admit this to you, dear Diary, and to nobody else, that one of the reasons I haven't touched my flute again is that I've always been scared my lips might have been damaged too much to let me play properly. I know there's probably no problem but deep down somewhere in what passes for my brain there is that thought. Maybe that's one reason why I don't talk any more too, huh? Who knows? This is riddle time.

I lay in bed last night wondering what it would have been like if I had swapped parents in the cradle. Perhaps I should have wrapped myself up and put myself on the Lindells' doorstep. They seem to me like they would have been pretty cool parents. It seems stupid to envy little kids as young as theirs, but I envy them, I sure do.

April 25

Term ends in one week. It's Cathy's birthday in four days. It's my birthday in six weeks: I'll be fifteen. It's exactly eight months till Christmas. Today is Anzac Day and Lisa and Rikki Martin had to go to a service somewhere on behalf of Year Nine. I feel restless and impatient today, which is unusual for me. I spent the session with Mrs Ransome zipping and unzipping my pencil case, which must have driven her crazy, but she didn't say anything.

April 26

Tonight at roll call Mrs Graham found out a girl called Sally Judge, in Year Eight, had run away. There was mass panic! Prefects went off in all directions to search and they soon figured out that she had gone because her overnight bag and some of her clothes were missing. Mrs Graham absolutely cracked a mental. They decided she must have gone after afternoon classes, but somehow no-one noticed, or else her friends covered for her, right through Sport, tea and Prep. Mrs Graham said if anyone had helped her they would be in deep trouble and she raved on about how dangerous it was and how Sally might have been sold to white slavers or rented out to Hell's Angels or something. But what I keep thinking about is why she would have run away and how she must have been unhappy and how Mrs Graham didn't say anything about that and didn't seem to care about it. And more than anything I wished I had got to know her, or at least taken notice of her. I wonder if she was like me, for instance? It didn't occur to me that there might be other people here who are feeling really bad. Little dark islands floating in the shadows of the school, occasionally touching, bumping together for a moment or two. I suppose she'll come back here and I'll look at her and wonder about her, but it'll be different then because everyone'll notice her and she'll be out there in the light. I'm not sure why that should make a difference, but it does.

I wonder where she is tonight, if she's safe, if she's lonely and cold and scared, if she wishes she was back here, if she's staying with friends maybe? I went to the chapel for a while and sort of prayed for her (well, I sat there and thought about her anyway, and hoped she was all right).

April 27

No news of Sally Judge tonight and already, after the first rush of feeling yesterday and this morning, people seem to be forgetting. Not forgetting exactly, but not thinking or talking about her so much. Emma says she ran away because her family is moving to America and she doesn't want to go, but I don't know how she knows that.

Just after I wrote that paragraph, Miss Curzon, the house tutor, came in and told us that Sally had been found — that she'd turned up at her grandmother's place in the country somewhere. They were the only details she had, even though everyone was firing questions at her. It was a relief and I was pleased that she was OK, but then I got worried about how much trouble she'd get into at school and whether she'd be allowed back. I hope she is.

There's still about twenty minutes to go in Prep and I can't think of anything to write. Sophie's been humming 'Can't Get Nothing But Love' all through Prep and driving everybody mad. Lisa's in a really over-the-top mood, cracking poor jokes and laughing like a maniac. Cathy's writing to her boyfriend and Kate's telling her what to write, but all of her suggestions are totally pornographic. Now Sophie's starting in on me again. I think she does it when she's bored — it's like she switches from Prep, to a novel, to me, to letter writing. I'm just one of many diversions for her. All I can do is keep my head down and keep writing here, acting like I'm not bothered. She keeps asking me why I don't speak, for Chrissake. I DON'T KNOW, FOR CHRIST'S SAKE. SO SHUT UP, SHUT UP, SHUT UP.

April 28

Mrs Graham told me that my mother would pick me up for the school holidays on Tuesday afternoon. She was in a hurry and that's all she told me, so I don't know anything else, but I expect I'll be staying with my mother for the whole time. I wonder if I'll be going into the hospital again?

Ann's going to Japan for her holidays.

Tomorrow's Cathy's birthday. I don't know what to do about it: I don't know if I can do anything about it, but she's been so kind to me and I admire her so much. Last night, for instance, I think she knew I was upset after Prep and she brought me a cup of Milo when I was getting ready for bed. Sometimes it seems like I go for weeks on end being totally ignored by everyone, and then Cathy comes along and does something like that and I feel like I'm in a shattered, shocked heap of little pieces on the floor, trying to put myself and everything back together into the new pattern — everything having to be reconstructed in a slightly different way.

April 29

Well, I did it! I did it! I gave Cathy a card and a present from my own hand, handed it to her after tea, and then ran away and shook under my tree for half an hour. That was pretty good for someone who hasn't done any thing like that for over a year! The present wasn't much — I made a little creature (like a wombat I guess) out of seeds and nuts and stuff that I picked up around the grounds this morning. It was something that I saw them doing in Occupational Therapy. But the hardest thing was giving it to her. I was going to leave it on her bed, but I forced myself to slide up to her and hold it out for her to take. Then I ran away before I could see what her reaction was.

Also, I forgot to say, after Sport this morning Mr Lindell came and found me and gave me some cookies that his wife had sent. How nice is that?

And, furthermore, also, again, Sally Judge came back today. I watched her during tea. She seemed very quiet, rather pale, though she laughed a few times as she sat there among her friends. I thought she looked nice. She's very pretty. But at roll call last night Mrs Graham said she was selfish to have run away. I think that's a dumb attitude.

So here I am, sitting at my desk, writing in this journal, eating the cookies Mrs Lindell made, about to go to the movie. I guess it's been a pretty good day!

9.15 PM:

When we were coming out of the movie Lisa came up to me and put her arm around me as I walked along and said something like: 'That little creature you gave Cathy was so sweet. I read the card too — I hope you don't mind.' I was just fading into the stars of the night sky with embarrassment, dying, dying, dying, even as my feet kept moving. Then Lisa said: 'Cathy cried when she opened it, did you know?'

I didn't know. I'm not sure that I wanted to know. When she opened what — the parcel or the card? Lisa didn't say, and I'm still not sure. All I wrote on the card was: 'I hope you have a Happy Birthday and I wish you love.'

It's been quite a day. I'm going to bed.

April 30

I was sort of scared of everyone and embarrassed all day, but then I wanted to be around them too, for once — partly because I'm scared about these holidays. I'd rather be here than at home with my mother and stepfather. I'm not saying I like this place at all — I don't — but there are worse places to be and there's a sort of warmth in the air here most of the time that grows on you gradually. It beats the giant cube that my mother lives in. This afternoon Cathy gave me this note. She put it in my hand, and I took it, then got away as fast as I could, to read it:

Thank you for the present and the card. I was really touched when you gave it to me, because none of us knows if you like us or not. But you seem happier lately: we've all noticed that.

I want you to have this poem that I wrote about you a month or so back. I hope you like it and it doesn't upset you or anything.

Pale as ice you passed me by;
I wondered what you really felt,
And waited through the changing times,
To see if you would one day melt.

I thought that ice would melt with warmth,
But there were things I did not know:
The sun can touch the outer layers
But does not reach the deepest snow.

Winter sometimes seems like years,
Summer's sometimes far away,
But winter always turns to summer,
As surely as does night to day.

One thing I wonder about sometimes. Would my mother ever go visit my father? I guess not. Does my father get any visitors at all? Would I ever go visit my father?

May 1

It's the end of term tomorrow. It's come with such a rush. No Prep is being done. Everyone's packing and there's flurry and fluster everywhere. 'Flurry and Fluster' — sounds like a pair of puppies. Cathy's going home to her country property and taking her honeyed mind with her. Emma's going home to Hong Kong. I'm happy for her. Lisa, I guess, is going home too. I don't know. She's so reserved. Tracey's going to Surfers Paradise with her parents. Kate's staying with Sophie for the first week. Ann's going to Japan, like I mentioned before.

Cathy came over to me a while ago in the dorm while I was packing and said: 'Where are you going for the holidays?' She seemed really nervous. I couldn't answer of course; I turned away and kept folding clothes, hardly knowing what I was doing. I was nearly crying, but I controlled it, and didn't let her see. I wanted someone to feel sorry for me because I don't want to go with my mother. I hope she wasn't offended. I hope she didn't think I was snobbing her or something.

I think I'll take this journal with me.

I wonder who'll pick me up tomorrow, and what time and everything? It's pretty scary — I mean, I wish I knew more. Mrs Graham hasn't told me much.

I don't feel very well. I've been coming down

with something for the last few days, I think. I ought to go to sick bay, but how do I explain anything to Matron? Guess I'll go to bed.

May 5

I walked into the city today. It's the first time I've been out since the holidays started, except for the first day, when my grandmother took me back to her place for tea. So I headed off, trying to walk normally, so as not to look too conspicuous, and before long I found myself in a street at the east end of the city that looked vaguely familiar. I still don't know the name of it even now; I don't know the city too well. It took only a few moments to work out why it looked familiar, because I suddenly found myself outside the Family Court buildings. That was where it all started. Oh, it didn't all *start* there of course but, it was the place that brought it all to a head and it was the judge's ruling in that big gleaming building that sent my father so totally off his brain. I felt a bit nauseous standing there. I wondered yet again how much of it was my stupid fault; how much the things I said to the judge had influenced the case. Guess I didn't like my father much at that stage of my life.

Just seeing that building made me feel so bad I gave up on my walk and headed on back here. I'm glad I've got this journal with me. But it's hard for me to write in it here: this doesn't seem the place for it. My mother's ignoring me. I think she's so disgusted that I still don't talk after a whole term at Warrington that she's given up on me.

May 6

They're all here today; the place is full of people. So I'm staying in here (I'm in my bedroom) doing nothing in particular, keeping out of sight. I wish I was at the Lindells' again. I was thinking of writing to them, because I never said 'Thank you' to Mrs Lindell. Maybe I could send a present to Anna.

May 7

God, I hate it here. I wish I was dead. I keep trying to figure out ways of killing myself. I've got to see Dr Harvey on Tuesday. Maybe he'll re-admit me. I know I'm not doing so good any more. But what the hell ... even the hospital would be better than this.

May 8

Oh joy! Oh jubilation! Today a wonderful thing happened. A letter from Cathy! What is it with her? When my mother gave it to me my eyes swelled up and filled my face with shock. How did that girl get my address? I guess she must feel sorry for me. She's crazy!

This letter now takes its place in my journal:

'Moonibah',
Tregonning.
May 4.
Dear friend of the silent voice,
Hi! How are you? I'm sitting in a little garden behind the house, writing this in the afternoon sun. It's my second day at home and so far I've filled my time by sleeping, sleeping, making friends with my horse again, and sleeping. The best fun's been making friends with my horse again. But it's all been good. The first few days of the holidays are always good, because everyone's so pleased to see you, and there's the pleasure of rediscovering everything and seeing the little changes.

Here are the little changes I've noticed: there's new wallpaper in the bathroom, very beautiful, trees and exotic birds and flowers on a cream background. It makes the room so airy and cool, though Dad says we should have had a design with gum-trees. Mum's favourite butcher has closed down so now she has to go to the other one, which she's not too happy about. Dad's got a new header: it's about as wide as the paddocks: it's enormous. It's got a tape player, so now he can listen to his Beatles' tapes in peace. What else? The hairdresser in town's pregnant and (SCANDAL) not married. My little brother's about thirty centimetres taller ... well, that's a slight exaggeration ...

It's been good being able to sit down and talk to my parents again. I'm so lucky — they're so easy to talk to and they always seem to understand. I miss them so much when I'm away at school. I've told Mum about you and she said you should come and stay. What do you think about that? I never know whether to press you or not. I guess I bombed out on the last night of term, when I tried to speak with you. I'm sorry about that.

Well, better go I guess. Hope you're OK. See you soon. Lots of love,
Cathy.

May 12

I finally wrote back to Cathy tonight. All I wrote was:

Dear Cathy,
Thank you very much for your letter. I'm sorry I didn't write straight away but I've been back in the hospital for three days now. I got re-admitted Wednesday. I don't think they're going to let me back to school next term, because I didn't start talking or anything like I was meant to, so I think I have to stay in here. Your letter was so nice, the nicest thing that has happened to me these holidays.

It took ages to write. Now I'll have to get a stamp somehow, I guess from Sister Dass. I don't know what the procedure is for letters. I've never written one from here before.

May 13

It's not good being back here. I'm not proud about it. I thought I was doing OK, until the holidays anyway. Not great, but OK. There's virtually no-one here that I know from last time — except staff of course.

It's hard to get a few minutes of privacy just to write in this journal.

Everyone seems to put such a big premium on whether I speak or not. Why's it such a big deal? I don't understand that. Seems to me that words just cause a lot of misunderstandings. 'When your mouth's open, you're not learning anything.' I don't say a lot (well, I don't say *anything*) but I notice plenty.

I wonder if HE and my mother had me put in here to get me out of the way?

May 14

Dr Harvey has found out about this journal and wants to read it. THERE IS NO WAY IN THE WORLD. I will *burn* it rather than let him read it.

May 15

Here is the final draft of my letter that I have sent today to Mr Lindell:

Dear Mr Lindell,

I am writing to you because you are the only person I know who might help me.

I have been put back in hospital here since last week and they say I may not be coming back to school because they don't think I've made any improvement. Mr Lindell, I want to come back to school like everyone else at the start of term next week. I think it is the best place for me. I know I don't talk, but I have other voices, like writing in my journal. I have started to like Warrington, and if I don't go back there, then what is to become of me?

I am sorry about writing to you but I need help.

May 16

I never thought I'd cry in this hospital but today I did. A nurse came towards me with a big bunch of flowers wrapped in cellophane, from a florist. She held them out to me and I didn't understand what was happening. Then I gradually started realising they might be for me. I took them away into my room. Luckily no-one was there. They were from Cathy. I buried my face in them and cried and cried. She has even written to the head-mistress about me:

> Get well quickly. I hope you're back at school next week.
> With love from Cathy and the Preshill family.

May 18

Mr Lindell is here! I just saw him walking down the corridor with Dr Harvey. He was quite a way off but he saw me and waved. I stopped and gaped, and then smiled at him. Sister Dass was going past and she nearly fainted. She said: 'I didn't know you could smile.' Well, I didn't either. But what's he doing here? What's going on? It's too exciting!

5 PM:
Mr Lindell has gone again but he came and talked to me. He said he'd called on my mother first, then he came to the hospital. He said it's OK and I'll go home tomorrow and to school on Tuesday. He gave me a hug and I started crying again. Then Dr Harvey came in (he left just a few minutes ago) and said it seemed like I was making more progress than he'd realised, so I should keep going to school. This has not been a red letter day but a red word one.

May 24

Well, here I am in Prep again. We've been back just over 24 hours. When I saw the muck we got for tea tonight, I thought, 'Why did I bother?' And now that I'm in another long, boring Prep session I know I was crazy. But, here I am. And everyone seems friendly. It was even OK to see Sophie again. She grinned at me when I came in last night and said: 'Hiya, Marcel.' Marcel, huh! Marcel Marceau, that French mime artist, I guess. I remember her saying last term how she'd been taken to a Marcel Marceau performance at Christmas and how she'd farted loudly right in the middle of all that silence.

Cathy got in just after me. Her mother was with her, having driven her back. In they came with luggage and food and teddy bears and stuff. It was good to see Cathy. I couldn't help but smile and she looked really pleased when I did. She introduced me to her mother, who was so nice, and invited me to stay next mid-term. I just blushed and smiled and looked away and got a few tears in my eyes too, I guess. I wonder if she meant that — about staying with them?

Then, Lisa. After school today I was in the dorm on my own when she came in. She stopped by my bed and said: 'You OK? You need anything?' I shook my head and she smiled and said: 'I really just wanted to tell you that I'm glad you're back, OK?'

One day I'll tell her how terrible I felt the day she was crying and I couldn't do anything about it.

It was good to get away from my mother and stepfather again too. The last few days of the holidays back at their place were terrible. I felt like I was all raw and every time I came near them it was like having a harsh hot radiator turned on me. I found myself wishing (I'm ashamed to say this) that my father's aim had been better after all, and that he had got her instead of me, like he'd planned. I tried imagining how she would have screamed and staggered away and how her expensive face would look now.

I still don't know what to do about him — about my father, I mean. I don't think I could ever visit him. But sometimes I think about writing him a letter. I don't imagine anyone else is going to. A couple of days ago, at home, I was reading a newspaper and there was an article in it about some guy who was being sentenced for a sex crime with little kids, and it said that men who've hurt children get a really bad time in prison from the other prisoners. I went to the bathroom and threw up. I can't stand to think of him in there on his own, getting punished so badly and feeling so desperate. Nobody understood him, least of all my mother. He just went mad because he'd worked so hard to get everything and then she was going to take it all off him and walk away with it, just like that, really cool. He couldn't have stood for that. He would have snapped. He was too proud; that's what she'd never managed to figure out about him. He would never have wanted to hurt me, not the way he did. I mean, there were a few times when he belted me and stuff, but only when he was really angry and half the time I'd provoked it by being rude or lazy or something. I know he wasn't the perfect father exactly — I wish he'd been able to hug me more and be warm and funny and happy, like other kids' fathers — but I do sort of miss him, in a way. Maybe I could go off to the judge and ask them to let him out. If it was me asking they'd have to consider it.

May 25

Kate launched into lurid stories of her holidays last night. She says she lost her virginity one night at a dance, when she was too drunk to do anything about it. I never know whether to believe her or not. Emma's got braces: she looks like she spent half the holidays at the orthodontist. Ann's not back from Japan yet.

Right now, as I write this, Kate's having a fight with Lisa because Lisa's captain of the netball team and she's put Kate in the team for Saturday and Kate wants to go on leave. I don't know what the fuss is about: it's really up to Dr Thorley, the coach. Emma's not talking to Sophie because she says Sophie owes her money from last term but Sophie claims she paid her back.

And Tracey's still annoyed with me from this morning because she said I stayed in the shower too long and used all the hot water.

So, this is where I am, on this night, May 25, eleven days from my fifteenth birthday, sitting in the Prep room of Year Nine dorm B at Warrington. And this is where I wanted to be. Today was a ratty day. Tomorrow could be the same, or worse. Or it could be better. Whatever, it was my decision, and I can live with it. It feels good. It feels right for me. It's a long way from the sleep to the dream. But I'm still in with a chance. It's like Mr Lindell said in class today: 'The darker the night, the brighter burns the candle.'

One day I'll walk right up to him and actually speak, out loud, and I'll say ... I don't know ... what'll I say? I often think about it. 'The rain in Spain falls mainly on the plain'? 'That's one small step for man'? 'Sally sells sea-shells ... '? I don't know. Probably something boring like: 'I haven't done my homework, sir.'

I often picture the look on his face.

I'm going to the Lindells' again this week. He asked me today.

Time I went to bed. Lights are out in a minute.

May 29

It's funny about a face, how big a difference it makes. I mean, one day you look in a mirror and you think, yeah, that's me, that's my face. And then another day you sneak out of your room, when the nurses are at tea, and you find a bathroom and go in and look in the mirror (you have your hands over your eyes but you peep through your fingers) and you think, that's not me, that's not my face. So am I my face? I mean, is that *all* I am? I don't know the answer to that but I do know that, because part of my face is changed, I'm not the person I was before. I'm a different person. I don't know who, but a different one. Once I tried to tell myself that it's who you are inside that counts, but that didn't work too well because I knew I'd changed inside anyway.

But even if I hadn't ... what I mean is, if my big toe had changed radically, or my kneecap, or my bum, it might upset me but I'd still be the same *person*, wouldn't I? That's not true of my face. Because it has changed, the person I once was is lost and gone forever. I miss her, but she has slipped away like a spirit and has disappeared into a land of spirits, and she will never never return.

May 30

I had a good time at the Lindells' last weekend. I wasn't too nervous. The first time it was exciting because it was all so new; this time it wasn't so exciting but it had a nice familiar feeling to it. I loved seeing little Anna again — God, she's so sweet! I hope nobody ever does anything to hurt her or destroy her innocence. They will, of course, but not if I can stop them first. I'd kill anyone who hurt her.

We went down the street Saturday morning and Mr and Mrs Lindell left Anna with me while they took the boys into Woolworths to get some stuff. I mean, they just left her with me! Pretty dangerous, I thought — what could I have done if anything had happened? But I felt proud that they'd trusted me that much. We window-shopped along the street for a bit while we were waiting, Anna chatting away non-stop, as usual. Then, quite suddenly, out of nowhere, we had a crisis on our hands. We'd paused at a pet shop, where they had cages and stuff in the windows and out on the footpath, with animals and birds in them. I thought she might enjoy looking at kittens and puppies, and that kind of jazz, like little kids are supposed to. But not Anna. First she didn't like the fact that they were in cages at all. Then she decided that one of the puppies was sick. Before I knew it, she was in the shop and dragging this lady out to have a look. If it came to that the poor little thing did seem a bit out of it, shivering away in a corner on his own. For all I knew he probably had foot and mouth disease. Anyway, there I was, dying of embarrassment and expecting this lady to abuse either Anna or me or both of us at once. But she didn't really; she just said 'Yeah, he does look a bit crook,' and took him out of the cage. Anna wanted to touch him of course; I guess she thought she was entitled, seeing as how she'd saved his life and all, but the lady said 'Better not, dearie,' and carried him back in the shop, and that was the end of it. So I guess it wasn't exactly a crisis, although at the time it seemed like one to me. But what amazed me about it all was just the innocence and honesty of Anna. I mean, little kids really are incredible. I figured that, after we left, the woman probably put the dog right back in the cage or else chucked it in their private gas chamber or something, but I don't think that thought would have occurred to Anna in a million years. She sort of trusts people automatically and she takes it for granted that they're all good.

Sunday we went for a picnic — about an hour's drive, up into the hills. It was nice, nice, nice. Stuart made himself a sandwich out of chocolate mousse and peanut butter, then had an argument with Scott and smeared the sandwich all over him when their parents were looking at a tree on the other side of the park. And after lunch the two boys had a spitting competition, where each had to let the other one spit in his face, without blinking. Pretty off, huh? But they were both so funny. They're cute kids, but boys can be disgusting sometimes.

Mrs Lindell told me she thought I was looking better. Maybe I am. I guess I was smiling a few times during the weekend. She made me some cookies to bring back here with me.

May 31

Sophie fell out of a tree last night and sprained her ankle and cut her head open. So now she walks with a big limp and has a bandage around her head, and they call her 'Hop-a-long Lobo'.

June 2

It's another weekend at Warrington. A big yawn goes up all around the school. Everyone was moaning tonight about how they all wished they were day-girls. But this weekend looks a bit better than some because they're doing auditions for the school play tomorrow afternoon. I might sneak in and watch from the back. The play is a thing called *Flowers for Algernon*. I don't know much about it, but there's meant to be a part in it for a rat, or so Mr Lindell said in class today. I might try out for that. Cathy and Lisa and Sophie are all going for parts, and maybe Kate, who keeps saying: 'Oh, do you think I should?' in a really annoying voice, obviously wanting everyone to say: 'Oh yes, Kate, you'd be good.'

Oh. That's funny. No sooner had I written that than Lisa turned around and said: 'Kate, you're only fishing for compliments. Make up your own mind.' Wow! Maybe we're telepathic. Anyway, that shut Kate up. I admire the way Lisa can say things like that to people.

All the main parts will go to Year Twelves, I imagine, unless they're busy with their exams. If that's the case then it'll be Year Elevens.

The male roles are being taken by boys from Grammar — a very daring move for Warrington (although it's the same every year, apparently).

Oh, there's so much to write! Actually the dorm is getting on *really* well at the moment, in spite of what Lisa said to Kate a minute ago. There's been virtually no arguments and everyone seems happy and friendly towards each other — even to me. They're all looking forward to snowfalls in the Alps because they're all keen skiers, except Tracey and Emma. Well, good luck to them. That's another thing I used to enjoy. My mother wasn't all that keen but my father was, so I used to go quite often. He belonged to two ski lodges. I wouldn't say it was totally great, because he left me to my own devices a lot of the time, or arranged for me to hang round with other families, or other kids, or go to the ski school, and there were times when it got a bit boring, but overall I would have to say I enjoyed it. And I did get to be quite a reasonable skier.

This term's got a different feel to it; I don't know why. I've trapped myself a bit, because I said I wanted to come back, so now, when I get sick of the place and start hating it, I have to remind myself that it was my choice to be here. I think I set myself up a bit. People are accepting me better though. And I walk along pretty normally now, not shrinking into the walls. And I hand some work in to be marked, when I can do it inconspicuously. The biggest difference though is that, in the dorm, people include me somehow, in a way that they didn't do before. It's not just Cathy, though I guess she started the trend. Last night, when they were talking about skiing (it was during Prep, so everyone was whispering) Cathy asked me, just normally, as though she were talking to anyone: 'Have you ever been skiing?' and I nodded a 'Yes'. Then she said: 'Are you any good?' and I shrugged, feeling embarrassed, but pleased too, at the attention. Then Sophie said: 'Wait a minute. I remember you. You were in Wonnangatta Lodge, about three years ago. I remember you! You were a hot skier!'

Well, I didn't know about that. Wonnangatta

was my father's lodge on Mount Buller, but I couldn't remember Sophie. But I smiled anyway ... and, dearest journal, that's called COMMUNICATION, and it made THREE different types in about sixty seconds — a nod, a shrug and a smile — and THAT is a WORLD RECORD!

Anyway, during supper break, I heard Sophie say to Cathy: 'I'm sure it was her. She was really pretty. My brother had a dance with her at a disco that they organised one night for kids.'

And then I remembered.

June 3

Winter sport hasn't really started properly yet so the weekends are free. And this morning Cathy took me for a walk down to the beach. She said she'd go through all the routines about asking for leave and stuff, and so she did, and so we went. It was pretty exciting for me! I felt like one of the agoraphobia ladies at the hospital, taking their little walks out into the grounds for the first time. It was a cold day, so we weren't about to go swimming or anything, but it was nice walking along the sand, although I was terribly nervous at first, because I didn't know what Cathy expected of me. For that matter, I still don't know. Was I meant to entertain her, the way friends seem to? Was I meant to laugh and tell jokes and exchange gossip and tap-dance and juggle live jellyfish? Well, I didn't do any of those things. Cathy talked a bit, which was all right, but it made me feel a bit helpless, because I wasn't doing anything in return. But after a while she stopped talking and we just wandered along in a really casual way. Cathy picked up a stick and started drawing huge messages in the sand, mainly about some boy she'd met in the holidays. Guy, his name is, and she really likes him.

While she was doing that, I picked up a little stick and drew messages too ... little tight messages as I sat on the sand. I drew lots of stripes, which weren't stripes at all, but were bars, prison bars.

You see, one of the reasons I couldn't write to him is that I wouldn't know how to start the letter off. I mean, there's only three possibilities really: 'Dear Father', 'Dear Daddy' or 'Dear Dad'. I don't think I could use any of them. The first one's too formal, the second one's too childish and the third one's too friendly.

The other day Mr Lindell read us a poem written by a man whose father had died. When he was cleaning out the house, this man found, in a drawer, a whole lot of poems his father had written, that he'd never known about. And he was saying how sad it was that his father had had this hidden side to him that he'd never known about and now it was too late to get to know him better. And I thought, all you'd find in my father's papers would be financial statements and share certificates and lists of figures.

After we got back from the beach I sneaked in and watched the auditions. It could be a pretty good play! It's about this man who's mentally retarded until they invent some radical technique that makes him a genius. He gets so smart that he's able to analyse his own treatment, and identify a fault in it that no-one else has seen, and he realises that the changes in him won't be permanent — that in a little while he'll degenerate to being mentally retarded again. He has a pet rat too, that the doctors have been experimenting on — that's where the rat that Mr Lindell mentioned comes into it.

None of the kids in our dorm seemed to do brilliantly at the audition, but Lisa was pretty good, and so was Sophie, surprisingly. But there was a Year Twelve, a girl called Nikki Loton, who was stunning — she had everyone in the hall totally absorbed. She'll get the main female role for sure, I think.

June 5

Ho hum, another boring night in Prep. I spent the whole of the first half trying to work out the Maths homework and still didn't get anywhere. We're doing Geometry this term. I thought it'd be easy, but it isn't. That's one of the problems with being silent and all, you've got to do everything on your own. Oh for a lighthouse on a deserted coast! Just me and the birds, and the waves crashing on the rocks. Kate's way of doing Maths Prep is to borrow Lisa's book and copy it all out. God knows what happens when it comes to exams. I guess she tries to sit next to Lisa.

Ann got back from Japan yesterday. She sure missed a lot of school. She came in all kind of lively and confident, more so than usual. I guess she was excited to be back. She brought presents for all of us — just little things, but sweet. She even had one for me: a kaleidoscope, with all those endlessly changing patterns, each one beautiful in its own way, each one unique. She gave Cathy a Japanese doll, and Kate a poster of a Sumo wrestler, which seemed a bit tactless — but I don't think Kate got the joke.

Ann learns Japanese at school — half the girls in the dorm do — so she'll probably be a bit of a star at it now, I suppose.

June 6

Today's session with Mrs Ransome, the counsellor, was quite different. I was getting so used to things floating along in the same old way when I was in there that I hardly noticed the sessions any more. I pretended not to be taking any notice, as always, but of course I was. She said I

107

needed to resolve my feelings about my parents and myself and until I did I wouldn't make much progress; that my silence and all that was because there were things about me and them that were so painful I couldn't face them; that my dread of the 'cure' was so bad that I was running away from it rather than enduring the pain of going through it. She said the 'cure' involved looking at feelings that had been too frightening for me to think about, like whether my parents maybe hated me, whether I maybe hated them, whether I maybe hated myself. She said parents are so important in a kid's life that if the kid feels rejected by her parents it's hard for her then not to think that everyone in the world is going to reject her.

Well, God, I listened to this stuff closely, I can tell you, though it set wild birds beating their wings in a flurry inside my chest and produced a bad dry lump somewhere round the top of my throat. I was a bit surprised too, because I guess I'd been discounting Mrs Ransome a bit in my mind, especially after that comment that I heard the Sister in the sick bay make about her, way back last term. I hadn't realised she was so perceptive. I don't know whether I liked the fact that she was that smart, either. I don't know whether I liked my defences being penetrated so suddenly.

Anyway, she went on to say that eventually I'd need to figure out both the good and bad elements in my relationships with my father and my mother and my stepfather; that there would be both love and hate in my feelings towards them, and I needed to look at both sides. That seemed to me — and it still does now, writing this — to be a bit of an impossible dream. However ... What I did do though was the first active thing I've ever done in there ... I took a thick felt pen and drew a picture on her nicely painted wall. To her credit she didn't even blink. It was like the picture I'd been drawing on the beach, a head behind bars. 'Is that your father?' she asked, quite gently, but I shook my head. 'Is it you?' and I shook my head again. I couldn't figure out any way to show her but after a while she got it anyway. 'Is it both of you?' and I nodded.

June 7

Well, today it was, dear Diary, my birthday, fifteen years old, never kissed and never likely to be (except for a few pretty pathetic dates in Year Six). The worst thing was that everyone knew, after I'd been feeling smug and confident for weeks that there was no way they could. I think Mrs Graham told them — she might have got it from the school records, because when she inspected the dorm after breakfast she certainly showed she knew about it.

I remember writing in here before that the

worst torture imaginable would be to be tied up and have to listen to people paying you compliments. Well, today was a bit like that. It was painful but nice — 'bitter-sweet', like the name of that old movie. It got a bit much for me though and I started kind of huddling into corners and shrinking into walls again, till I think they realised that they were overdoing it and turned the spotlight down again.

But, while it lasted, there was something nice about it. They sang me 'Happy Birthday' of course, all in daggy voices, trying to be funny — that was as soon as I woke up in the morning, when I was still in bed — and they all had presents to give, which was probably the hardest part of all. There was some perfume from Sophie, books from Tracey and Emma, a pen in the shape of a banana from Kate, an address book from Ann, a tape (*High-rise Clouds*, by Genetic Defects) from Lisa. Cathy gave me a jar of honey from their own hives; I remember her saying that her mother kept bees. And she'd made a card to go with it that was so beautiful. God she's talented!

After school there was a parcel from my mother — new jeans and a white blouse, Edwardian but not too frilly. I quite like it, really. And my grandmother sent a stack of food, including a cake. I put it out at supper tonight and kind of indicated that I wanted to share it, so we had a sort of low-key party.

All in all I'd say that if you have to suffer through a birthday, this wasn't a bad way to do it.

Nothing from my father though. Not that I expected anything.

June 8

Something funny happened today — well, not funny, *strange*. I went into the bathroom and Sophie was staring at herself in the mirror and, with her teeth clenched, she was saying to herself: 'I hate you, you off moll, you bitch.' It was like she was saying it over and over again, but then she saw me standing there and she ran off crying.

June 9

To my amazement I got a birthday present from Mrs Preshill (Cathy's mother) today. It was the softest and most beautiful towel I've ever seen — a deep burgundy colour, with white trimmings. But the biggest thing was the letter that came with it — it seems like they're serious about me staying there for the mid-term break. I don't know what to think. I don't think I could handle it all. But it was the nicest letter and it seems like she's taking it for granted that I'll come. She said she's writing to my mother, to get her approval. God, as if my mother'd mind! She'll be delighted to get me out of the way again.

Stacks of snow have been falling in the mountains, apparently, so all the skiers are excited. It's cold enough here, that's for sure.

Lisa and Sophie both got parts in the school play, but only little ones. Lisa's a nurse and Sophie's a woman who works in a bakery or something.

Had another session with Mrs Ransome. She said: 'Some of the questions you might like to think about are: "In what ways are you and your mother alike?", "In what ways are you different?", 'What do you like about yourself?".' I've forgotten what else she said. But I had a question ready for her. I had it written down on a piece of paper and I handed it to her when she'd finished talking. My question was: 'Can you get me an address for my father, please?' I didn't know whether I was ever going to write to him, or anything like that, but I thought it would be good to have ... in case. And besides, I just wanted to know where he was, so I could look it up on a map or something.

I was thinking tonight, after seeing the way Sophie was yesterday, in the bathroom, that maybe no-one's really happy; maybe underneath we're all the same. But I don't know. Tracey and Emma are happy people, I think. And Cathy certainly is, for all that she's deep and reflective. And I think Ann is. With Kate it's hard to tell; she's so wild and noisy all the time, although she's actually a bit quieter this term, come to think of it. That leaves Sophie, Lisa, and me.

June 10

My winter sport is softball, and it's the same deal all over again — I don't do anything. My name's at the bottom of all the lists, but I still have to go. This afternoon's match was at MLC, and playing in the team against us was Angela Wallis, who was in my class right through primary school, but I don't think she even recognised me.

June 12

Mrs Graham told us tonight that there's going to be a dance for Year Nines from four schools in three weeks' time, and one of the schools is Warrington. Everyone's so excited about it, 'cos any kind of contact with boys rates as a big deal round here. But I guess I never feel more left out of it than at times like these. My nightmare is that they'll make me go, that it'll be compulsory for boarders or something. If they try, I'll run away, I swear. I couldn't stand it.

I feel like I'm dropping a long way down again lately. There doesn't seem to be any special reason for it; I mean, everyone's a lot friendlier than they were last term. It's just me. I seem to be dropping into a cold dark wet place, where no-one's been before and no-one can ever follow. There's no future there; just a past that sometimes fools you into thinking it's the future. It's the most alone place you can ever be and, when you go there, you not only cease to exist in real life, you also cease to exist in their consciousness and in their memories. Writing about it doesn't help while I'm doing the writing but perhaps it helps afterwards. But it's not enough.

June 14

Got 27% in a Science test; not bad considering I didn't do any of the essay questions, just the multiple-choices (or multiple-guesses, as Mr Hardcastle calls them).

June 16

In First Prep tonight Lisa sent me a note, something that's not a regular event in my life, especially from Lisa, who seems to have kept out of my way this term. She wrote: 'You don't look too happy lately. What's going on?' I wrote back, in little writing: 'I don't know.' Then it sort of developed into one of those continuous backwards-and-forwards letter things, like a conversation, that the other kids have all the time during Prep, but that I've never been involved in before. It's the closest I've ever come to actually talking so far, I guess. Lisa's comments were a bit more extensive than mine, though. She's perceptive. I was scared at being involved in it but I didn't want her to stop either.

Lisa: *Is anyone giving you a hard time?*
Me: No.
Lisa: *Any teachers?*
Me: No.
Lisa: *Do you mind my asking you these questions?*
Me: No, it's OK.
Lisa: *Have you been feeling bad, like, worse than usual?*
Me: Yes, I think so.
Lisa: *Do you know why?*
Me: Yes, No. I'm not sure.
Lisa: *Are you worried that I'll tell the others, if you say anything to me?*
Me: No.

(That was true. I trusted her. She's very private but very strong.)

Lisa: *Is it to do with your face and your parents and all that?*
Me: Yes, I suppose, my father mainly.
Lisa: *Do you hate him?*
Me: No.

I realised that I didn't hate him at all, and tears started running down my face. It seemed like some sort of relief to know that. But they were silent tears and, the way our desks were positioned, I knew Lisa couldn't see them. I wrote a bit more:

> I don't hate him. I feel sorry for him. I'm scared about what might be happening to him.

That was the end of me then. I put my head on my arms and sobbed and sobbed. It was the first time anyone in the dorm had seen me cry properly, I guess. Lisa was holding me and saying 'I'm sorry, I'm sorry', like she was really scared. It took me a long time to get back to normal, but when I did, I wrote on the note: 'It's OK. I'm glad to get it out.' That eased her mind a bit. But I don't know if I *am* glad.

June 17

Went to the beach again with Cathy this morning. I felt pretty strange after last night but Cathy was cool, as always. We saw Miss Curzon strolling along with some guy way down the beach; I didn't know she had a secret lover. He'd have to be desperate. Cathy said she'd seen them at the movies last term, when she'd gone with some day-girls, and they bombed them with popcorn from the back stalls. God, who'd be a teacher!

Cathy just talked on, mainly about her family. She feels so close to them. She's got a brother. He's in Europe at the moment and she misses him a lot, even though he seems to be the wild one of the family. He had fourteen jobs in eight months when he was trying to save the money to go overseas. She said he went for one job with the RSPCA but missed out on it because he drove over one of their dogs in the driveway. I would have thought maybe they'd hire him after that. He worked in a meatworks and as a truckie's off-sider and as a fruit-picker. Then he worked in McDonald's for a while but they fired him after he told a customer that the hamburgers would make his coat shine. They take their food pretty seriously.

Cathy's family sounds nice; I like the way she's proud of her parents.

This afternoon our softball team played Girls' Grammar, at home, and beat them, which is good going, because no-one beats them at anything. I helped Sophie with the scoreboard — she still can't play, because of her foot. She can't add up either, but I don't think that's because of her foot.

June 19

Mrs Ransome came good with the address today. I was surprised. Bet she checked with some

20,000 people before she gave it to me. Dr Harvey, for one. Anyway, I've got it now: P.O. Box 259, Tarpaggi. She said he's in a place called Townley Prison Farm, but you don't have to put that on the envelope.

A prison farm. That doesn't sound quite as bad. I imagined him in a cell block, caged in concrete, having to fight mass murderers every day just to stay alive ... I mean, that makes it sound like I'm being funny, but I'm not. A prison farm might be all right, with fresh air and stuff, and I guess the prisoners wouldn't be so violent or dangerous there. I raced off to the library and looked Tarpaggi up in atlases and tourist guides and anything else I could find. It's in the foothills of the mountains, cold climate, light snow in winter; its industries are forestry and cattle grazing. Its population is only 200 and it looks an isolated place, but it's got to be better than some big inner-city gaol.

The dorm's really noisy tonight, but it's a happy kind of noise and I guess I can stand it. I think it's because Miss Curzon's on duty, but Mrs Graham came in a minute ago and told them they'd all be on detention if they didn't quieten down straight away.

June 20

Lisa has a card above her desk that she's written out in the last day or two: 'A LIFE UNEXAMINED IS NOT WORTH LIVING — *Plato*.' I like it. It makes me feel better about all the thinking that I do.

June 21

There's a lot of talk about this dance. Everyone's been ringing up friends in other schools to find out who's going. In two schools it's all the boarders, in one it's just the ones who want to go. Mrs Graham hasn't said with us, but Miss Curzon said it'll be all the boarders plus any day-girls who want to. So I don't know how I can get out of it. Maybe the Lindells will invite me there again. Tracey's making a dress for it in Needlework — I thought it'd be just a casual thing in jeans, but no-one seems too sure. Anyway, all I know is, I'm not going, even if the sky melts around me, even if the prince arrives with the glass slipper, even if the plastic surgeon turns up with laser beams and chloroform.

Lisa dropped Peter Fallon-White ages ago, so the relationship that never was, now never is and never will be, amen. Cathy and Andrew Lorimer drifted apart when Guy arrived on the scene, and I don't know about Sam and Emma.

Kate's talking about a different boy every week: I get confused. Ann's kind of quietly in love with a boy called Martin, but I don't know if that's his first name or his last name: she never talks about him. It'd be good if it was his last name and they got married — then she'd only have to change one letter in her name, from Maltin to Martin. (That's assuming girls still change their last name when they get married — I don't know any more.) Sophie's crazy about a boy from St Luke's, called Tom Dennis, but I bet he doesn't even know she exists.

Prep was hard tonight. I still can't figure out the Geometry, and there's a test next week, and exams soon. Tracey and Emma were drilling each other on French verbs all through First Prep, and they got really angry when everyone told them to shut up. They started saying how Sophie and Lisa and Kate rule the dorm and do anything they want, never caring how much it annoys others, and then when it suits them they go aggro on people who are doing exactly the same things. That's pretty true really, but Tracey and Emma are still at the bottom of the ladder in here (apart from me, and I'm not even on it) and so no-one takes much notice of them, and they know it.

Sometimes I wonder what would happen if I started talking and did play a full role in the life of the dorm. They'd all have to readjust to accommodate me, the new me, but I don't think they'd like it very much. In a way, everyone's comfortable with how it is.

'Everything changes, everything stays the same.' We have to write an essay for English, relating that to *Animal Farm*. God, he sets some hard topics! I don't know whether I'll write it on paper or just in my head.

June 22

I've got a sore throat (pretty ironic, seeing I hardly ever use it). Maybe I've got laryngitis and don't even know it. What a laugh. Swollen glands, Matron said. I'll have to go into sick bay if they get any worse. I wouldn't mind that; it'd be good to have a rest. Most of the school's in there already; you can hear them coughing when you're half way across the oval.

June 23

Just realised I haven't heard from my mother at all this term, except for my birthday. And I hadn't even noticed. But Cathy got a letter from her mother saying that she'd fixed it for me to go to the Preshills' for mid-Term break. Looks like these decisions are being made for me. I don't know if I want it or not.

My throat's still sore as hell. I've been sucking on Strepsils all day.

June 24

Well, here's what I finally came up with. It's not very good. In fact, it's pathetic. I solved the 'Dear Daddy' problem by not starting it with anything:

> I'm sorry I haven't written before. I hope it's not too bad where you are and that the food is good. It's not too bad here. I hope you're OK.

And that was all. It took two, nearly three hours to write that. Every other sentence I thought of, I immediately thought of a good reason for *not* putting it in, in case he took it the wrong way or something. So in the end I wasn't left with very much. I didn't know how to sign off, either ... I don't think I can sign it 'Love' or 'Your loving daughter' or even 'Yours sincerely'. The whole thing's just too difficult ... I'm going to chuck it away.

June 25

The bishop came to chapel today and took the service. He's surprisingly quiet for a bishop. The staff all fluttered around him, making a big fuss. But I guess it was no big deal for the students. He did say one thing though, when he preached the sermon, that stuck with me. He was saying how young people come to him looking for advice and stuff, and he sits there and listens to them talk about all their ambitions and what they want to do and what they want to be. And sometimes he has to interrupt them because they're getting really twisted up about it all, and he says to them: 'I've heard enough about what you want to do; now tell me what *needs* doing.' Pretty cute, hey?

All I have to figure out now is, what *does* need doing?

June 26

Well, I posted the letter today — stupid, but there it is, it's done now, even though I wanted to get it back as soon as I'd put it in the box.

Mr Lindell brought me in a chocolate cake that he said he baked himself. It's a bit boring though, with no icing. I think it's a packet one. This is what's called looking a gift horse in the mouth, I suppose. But there was also a note from Mrs Lindell inviting me to stay there for the mid-term break. I would have loved to do that but I guess I'm going to the Preshills'. And I guess I'm quite looking forward to that too.

June 27

Sophie, Kate and Tracey are in deep trouble yet again. It's a familiar place for them. They went on leave last weekend, supposedly to stay with

Tracey's older sister, but in reality to go up to the snow with two girls who got expelled from Year Twelve last term. They slept on someone's floor and in general had a wild raging time. But Trace's sister rang Mrs Graham this morning to ask if she could visit Trace after classes tomorrow, because she's going overseas next week and won't be seeing her kid sister in quite a while. And so the Bust of the Century was made by Mrs Graham and the three of them have been panicking around the dorm all evening. At the best they'll be gated until they're old women of fifty; at worst they'll be expelled. They won't find out till tomorrow though (the suspense is part of the punishment). I hope they don't get expelled; I guess I've come to like them as time's gone on.

Sophie ... well, what can I say? In the middle of all the panic and crying and everything Sophie turned to the others and said, with a big cheeky grin: 'Well, whatever they do to us, it was worth it!' And at that they all fell about on the floor laughing for five minutes, with pillows stuffed in their mouths in case Mrs Graham heard them. They would have been expelled on the spot if she had. I think Mrs Graham has trouble seeing the funny side of life sometimes.

No-one expects them to get expelled though — plenty of people have done worse things and not been kicked out.

June 28

Well, our three 'crims' got their punishments tonight — gated till the end of term, except for the mid-term break, of course . Already they're complaining like they've been hard done by, but everyone else thinks they're pretty lucky. Sophie'd complain if she'd been given a half-hour detention.

Of course one of the first things they will miss out on is the Big Dance, which I think is quite funny, but I'd never dare let them know that. They can take my place any time.

Mrs Graham gave the House a speech about trust, and how she's going to tighten up on leave from now on, and she's written to the parents of the three Year Nines, and she's writing to the ex-Year Twelves too, to warn them of the legal dangers they were putting themselves in by abducting these sweet innocent little children.

June 29

Oh God, for some decent food! Even the bread tonight was stale. We had rissoles with beans and mashed potato for the main course: the rissoles were dry and hard; the beans were soggy. If there was only some tomato sauce things wouldn't be all bad, but they wouldn't even provide that much. I came back here and made a hot drink with some of Cathy's Milo — hope she doesn't mind.

Mrs Ransome asked me today if I had written to my father. I just stared at that good old wall, still decorated by my great work of art, but I wasn't looking at that. I wasn't looking at anything, actually. But I didn't want to tell her what I'd done. I bet she reports everything straight back to the hospital.

Tracey pierced her ears tonight. As if her parents weren't going to be mad enough at her already! Maybe that's why she did it. She said it didn't hurt too much. Guess it'll be years before she reads another *Billabong* book. I think she just wants to keep up with Kate and Sophie.

June 30

Today has been a disturbing, frightening, confusing day. I don't know what to do. I have an answer to my letter already, within five days. I suppose I should have foreseen that that was possible but I had postponed any thought about it till way into the future. Anyway, here is the letter — like mine, with no greeting and no farewell:

Thank you for your letter. I am glad you wrote; more glad than I can say. I did not expect you to write.

I cannot say what is in my heart and anyway I do not

think I have the right. So I will write a little to you about my life here.

It is quite a good place, better than the first one I went to. It reminds me of parts of Europe, with extensive pine forests, very quiet and peaceful. Most of our work is in the pine forests, cutting and stacking and planting and so forth.

The men are not a bad bunch, though there are not many educated fellows among them. But some are allowed to go to the CAE in the nearest big town — Buntleigh — to do courses. So you see, we are quite trusted. I go in on the bus to the hospital every Monday for treatment for a hand I injured in the remand place. That is my day out, and I look forward to it.

You asked about the food. It is basic but there is plenty of it.

We play sport too. I am in the volleyball team and we play in a competition in Buntleigh. At some time I too will perhaps start a course at the CAE but we are only allowed one unaccompanied trip a week and, until my hand is fixed, that, of course, must take priority.

I imagine the life is not unlike that of a boarding school.

I will write no more now because I want this letter to catch this afternoon's mail. But I hope and pray you will write again to me very soon. I thank you once more for your letter.

Well, I have read it many times of course. I feel now that I have to write back, that I have committed myself.

It's almost like being trapped. In a way, I'd rather see him face to face. I can think of nothing that I can put in a letter. Oh, I don't know. His letter is so like him in so many ways. I'm worried about his hand. I've always been worried that he might have been attacked or something in prison. Think I'll go to bed and try to figure it out there. I hope he's OK.

July 1

Everything's looming close now. The Big Big Dance (it gets bigger the closer we get) is four nights away, and then the next day we go on mid-term break ... and I guess I'm off to the Preshills' at Tregonning, whether I like it or not. I like it, I guess — it's got to be better than going to my mother's. The real trouble is that I'm nervous — scared, frightened, terrified out of my brain. God, am I ever scared!

July 2

An inspiration hit me like a bomb in chapel this morning. I was sitting next to Cathy, imagining what it was going to be like going to Tregonning and staying on their property, when suddenly I remembered her saying how she got all her clothes and stuff for school in Buntleigh, because there were no big shops in Tregonning. Buntleigh was the nearest big town to my father. It was where he went for hospital treatment on his hand. I grabbed a pen and wrote Cathy a note in the back of the hymn book:

How often do you go to Buntleigh?

She wrote back:

About every three weeks.

I thought for a bit longer, then wrote:

Is there a bus from your place?

She answered:

No, train from Tregonning.

Could I go there while I'm staying with you?

Yes of course.

So I've spent the day in a pretty hyper mood. I mean, it probably won't come to anything, but the mere possibility has been enough to keep my mind in a state of epileptic excitement. It's hard to think about anything else — in fact I can't. I suppose I must really want to see him.

July 4

Gotta write this in a hurry — the place is in confusion, and I hate confusion. People are torn between packing for the mid-term break and getting ready for the dance tonight. That's those who are going to the dance, of course. Mrs Graham told me yesterday that if I didn't want to go I could watch TV in her flat. That was kind of her. Unexpected kindness is a shock — and this was unexpected. I thought she'd make me go to the dance. Sophie and Kate and Tracey have to do a two-hour detention and then go to bed. But they can laugh — they're all going skiing for midterm. So's Lisa. I still don't know about trying to get to Buntleigh on Monday, but I think about little else.

July 6

Well, I'm at 'Moonibah'. It's a relief to be able to draw a breath at last. It's the first breath I've had a chance to draw since I got here. Mrs Preshill picked us up at school at about three o'clock and brought us back here. She's one of those people who are competent at everything, always nice, never fazed, able to chat on in a pleasant and good-humoured way in any situation. Adults are amazing like that, with their confidence. Where does it come from? Do they acquire it automatically as they grow older? Are they given lessons when they leave school? Is there some secret that's being kept from me? I mean, I know there were adults in the psych. ward who couldn't handle it, who'd broken down, like scrap cars in the wreckers' yard, but they seem to be the exceptions.

Anyway, since we got here it's been non-stop. This seems to be another one of those magical families where people are nice to each other, and friendly and kind and generous. Mr Preshill didn't get in till after dark because he'd been mending a fence where the cattle had got through onto the road. That put him behind on some other work he'd been doing, building a new stockyard, so what does Cathy do the next morning — this morning? Gets up early and heads straight out to the stockyards to help. I went too, of course, but I was amazed by the way she did it so naturally, without feeling she had to do it, without feeling annoyed, without worrying about having a sleep-in or anything.

It was hard work too. I don't think I was much help. I started to regret letting myself get so unfit. We had to dig these hugely deep holes with a crowbar and shovel, then drop a massive log in, then start packing the earth back in around the log, again using a crowbar. Cathy was good at it but I was sore across the shoulders and in the arms in no time at all.

They want to get them done quickly because they have a big cattle auction on the property every year, and the next one's soon, and the yards aren't big enough any more. Cathy said the auction's their main source of income for the year, so it's important for them. Pays her school fees, I guess. Mr Preshill said the new yard was a bit of a waste of time because in a few years all the sales would be done by television and computer, but he didn't sound like he really believed that would happen.

Mr Preshill's so nice. He's a big man but you can see the resemblance to Cathy. His hair's pretty thin on top — there's just a few strands combed across the top of his head — but he's still quite fair. He talks very decisively and emphatically; when he tells you to do something you know exactly what he wants. But he seems very calm. You'd have to know him well before you could tell when he was angry, I think. He and Cathy seem to fit together so well — they never waste words when they're talking to each other — they just seem to know instinctively what each other thinks or wants.

I'm so glad I came here now! Even if nothing does happen on Monday. I still don't know what to do about that — but I think if I got so close and then did nothing I'd regret it for the rest of the year — the rest of my life, maybe.

July 8

I forgot to mention the Dance back at school. It seems like it wasn't the night of wild excitement that everyone was counting on. Cathy said there were more teachers than students and to go to the toilet you practically had to have a passport and visa and a personal note from the headmistress. But Cathy did OK — she met a boy and now she's writing his name all over her pencil case, with coloured stars, and stuff all around it. Stuart Dawson — he goes to St Luke's. I'm happy for her but I'm also jealous, I admit. I don't know what happened to Guy.

Cathy said that despite all the teachers there was still quite a lot of grog around, and some boys got busted in the car park selling Bundy. Today we did some more work on the stockyards, then went into Tregonning to do the week's shopping. I see now what Cathy meant about it being a small town. I stayed in the car — Cathy warned me that it takes half an hour just to buy a loaf of bread in Tregonning, because you have to stop and talk to everyone you see, and that didn't sound like my scene. She was right too — she met about ten different people before she was 50 metres down the street. Guess everybody knows everybody in Tregonning. But it seems a nice friendly town.

July 9

Well, it's all arranged for me to go to Buntleigh Monday if I want to. I feel pretty stupid writing notes to Cathy while I'm staying here but last night I wrote her a note just saying I'd like to go to Buntleigh Monday on the train.

'Do you want me to come?' Cathy asked, but I shook my head. I'd already thought about that. I hope she wasn't offended, but she didn't seem to be. 'OK I'll fix it,' she said. 'Dad has to go into Tregonning on Monday to get parts for the International. He could give you a lift.'

It's like rolling a rock downhill, I guess. Once you've rolled it, even if it starts a landslide, all you can do is stand and watch.

July 10

Cathy tried to get me to go riding today, first on a motor bike, then on a horse. I rode a trail bike a few times at a friend's place when I was a kid but now I don't seem to have the courage or confidence. But I gave in when it came to the horse, though I was terribly nervous. It was a quiet enough horse (not much more life in it than I've got) and it ambled around the paddock after Cathy's horse without any fuss. I don't imagine it would have moved at all if Cathy hadn't been there. I enjoyed it though. One day I'll gallop through the mountains, into the sunset, the biggest cliché in history — and loving it.

Mr and Mrs Preshill went to church this morning but we didn't have to go. I thought that was good. But we made the lunch and cleaned up the kitchen.

This evening I went for a little walk, before it got dark, watched the sun set, all that stuff. It was so so peaceful. This property, 'Moonibah', seems to me to be the most undisturbed place on earth. I leaned on a fence and looked across the valley. There were a few cattle that lifted their heads up occasionally to take a break from eating, and a rabbit that walloped across a paddock in a busy hurry, but nothing else much moved. I thought endlessly about tomorrow, of course. I knew there was a pretty good chance I'd see him — it shouldn't be too hard in a small country hospital, and I had all day. The most likely thing that could go wrong would be if for some reason he didn't come in at all — like, if his hand had healed. But if I did see him, what then? Would I just hide and watch without letting him know I was there? That was the most likely thing. But I wouldn't know until the moment came. I was scared about everything but I know what I'm most scared of — I've always known that. Scared that he'll hate me. Scared that he'll never forgive me for all the terrible and wrong things I've done these past fifteen months. I want him to hold me and forgive me and tell me it'll be all right, like I was six years old again. That's what I want. Maybe we could buy a farm like this one and live here happily ever after, away from the eyes and the voices of the people.

Tomorrow, tomorrow, tomorrow. I guess the Preshills aren't too impressed with me as a guest. Right now I don't want to be near anyone. All I can think about is what might happen in Buntleigh. I keep imagining him seeing me and then his face going cold and hard and him walking past me like I don't exist. His letter is the only thing that gives me the courage to go through with this. But letters and real life can be a long way apart. What people write and what they do and say when they're face to face needn't have much connection. I mean, look at my mother's letters — if you read those you'd think she really *liked* me.

July 11

Well, the day began this morning, as I heard a sports commentator say on TV once. Mr Preshill drove me to Tregonning, bought my ticket for me, asked me if I was OK for cash, gave me his sister's address in Buntleigh in case I got in any trouble, and told me about the return trains. I think he was a bit worried about me, but what I liked was, none of the Preshills asked me why I was going there, or anything. (Bit different to Mrs Graham at Warrington!)

It was a short journey — in one way anyway — and I got there just after nine, which was what

I wanted. Even from the station it was easy to pick out the hospital. There's something about them that sets them apart, like schools and prisons. It was half-way up a bit of a hill, a cluster of red roofs, big chimneys and car parks, with one big modern building extending out along the hill. I didn't know how I was going to figure out where to go when I got there, but it turned out to be easy — there was a series of big signs guiding the way to Outpatients, and that had to be the place he'd go to. It was in the modern wing, on the ground floor. I pushed open the big double doors and went in, trying not to look too tentative. After all, if there was anywhere I was going to feel at home, it was in a hospital.

The place was really crowded, even though there was a big waiting area. People looked at me curiously, or looked away in embarrassment, pretending not to notice. Before I walked more than three steps into the waiting room a sister intercepted me — which wasn't quite in my plans.

'Do you want to see a doctor?' she asked.

I figured the easiest thing would be to go along with that; otherwise more questions would follow. Besides, there were so many people waiting that if I put down to see a doctor I'd probably buy at least an hour or two in the place. So I nodded.

'OK, fill in the form please and take it to the desk.'

That was easy enough; at the desk they told me to sit down and they'd call me when my turn came. I sat down, nervously, in a corner, and began the vigil. I wouldn't say it was the longest wait of my life, because there have been a few others that rank pretty high, but it somehow seemed at least their equal.

I sat there thinking about the road I'd taken that had brought me to the Outpatients' clinic of a hospital in a town I'd hardly heard of a few weeks ago. The little girl I'd once been seemed a long way away now. God, when I thought how much I used to wish I was grown up! I used to do all the typical little girl stuff I guess, like dressing up in my mother's clothes and shoes. I had a photo my father took of me once when I was dressed up like that, but I haven't seen it in quite a while. I wonder what happened to it? I would imagine myself looking all glamorous and made-up, like my mother, smelling exotic and exciting. I had some really corny day-dreams, where I'd live in a big country house, with dozens of horses and servants, and hold huge dinner parties. Such corny stuff. When I was about eight I used to nag my father for a horse all the time, though it wasn't too practical an idea, considering where we were living then. He'd say 'Well, maybe, but not for a year or two', so I soon learned to give up on that one.

I don't know what's best really. I mean, he

worked so hard to make money so we could have things — skiing and clothes and nice houses and cars — but on the other hand I never got to see much of him, and he didn't get any time to enjoy all the things that he was buying. My mother did though — she had a great time. So I don't know what's best. I'd hate to be poor, but look where we've ended up after all his hard work — a family that's exploded, a father in prison, a mother who's married a creep and who cares only for herself, and a silent daughter with a face like raw mincemeat. I remember a poster that I saw on a railway station once — some religious group had put it up — and it said: 'No man is a success who is a failure in his own home.' So where does that leave my successful father?

The funny, sad, strange thing about it is that after all the disasters and hard hard times, the only person with whom I feel any real bond, the only one I think I maybe can somehow, some day, rebuild something with, is my father. I don't think there'd be a chance in a million of anyone else in the world understanding that — I don't even understand it myself — but there it is. I know I should hate him, but that night, when I swapped messages with Lisa, I realised I didn't. Maybe the acid nibbled its way through to my brain and wrecked my ability to think normally.

We're alike in some ways, different in others. We both find it hard — impossible — to show our feelings. I think I inherited his energy for hard work. (Well, I used to think that, but I don't know whether it's true any more.) We both like skiing and physical, outdoors sorts of things. But I think things through more deeply than he does. I used to believe I *felt* things more deeply than he does but I guess he's proved that that's not true. We both have terrible tempers but I've learnt to bottle mine up.

One of the worst things about everything is that I know he used to be quite proud of me when I was a little kid. I mean, he could never show that either, and he'd never say much in the way of compliments or anything, but I think he really was proud of me once. My mother even told me he was. But now ... losing that makes things hard to bear. And thinking about that, as I sat there on the hospital bench, my eyes started filling with tears again.

By the time I'd relived all those memories I'd been waiting there a good while and I was getting nervous that my name was going to be called, to see a doctor whom I had no reason to see, and whom I had no intention of seeing. If they did call me I was going to have to make a discreet exit from Outpatients. I'd seated myself in a corner from which I could see the main entrance clearly, but there were so many other entrances and exits that it was hard to keep track of the movement of people.

It was busy, for a country hospital. Every few minutes a sister would come to the door of the treatment area and call a name in a loud voice and the next patient would head over there. Each time I shrank further into my corner.

And then it all happened. The Sister came out of the treatment area for the hundredth time that morning, looked at a form in her hands, lifted her head and opened her mouth. I heard my name, pronounced clearly and unmistakeably for once, ringing out across the crowded benches. I panicked and stood up. To my right, behind me, there was a flurry of amazed movement (one can sense these things) from someone who had just come in a side door. I turned heavily, but knowing. He'd lost a lot of weight.

'Marina!' he said.

'Hello, Dad,' I answered.

Everything was still, the air swollen. My father, who never hugged, put his arms awkwardly around me. He felt bony and tight, but I knew this was hard for him. I held him as well as I could, wanting to say everything. We were both crying, I think. People were watching, and I was embarrassed, but I didn't want to let him go. We'd come quite a way to have this hug: it looked like being a long one.

I cleared my throat and tried again: 'I've got so much to tell you …'

About *So Much to Tell You*

This remarkable novel, now an established classic, is based on a true story. It was awarded the Children's Book Council Book of the Year in 1988, the Victorian State Premier's Award, the 1989 Koala Award and the Christopher Medal (USA), as well as being selected by the American library Association as a Best Book for Young Adults. It has been translated into nine languages.

About John Marsden

Over a million copies of John Marsden's books have been sold world-wide. In 1997 the *Australian* newspaper called him 'the most popular author today in any literary field'.

Since his first novel, John has written nineteen other books, including the young adult novels, *Letters from the Inside*; *Dear Miffy*; six books in the unprecentedly popular *Tomorrow When the War Began* series; and *Take My Word for It*, the sequel to *So Much to Tell You*. John has also written three highly sucessful and innovative picture books: *Prayer for the Twenty-first Century*; *Norton's Hut*, illustrated by Peter Gouldthorpe; and *The Rabbits*, illustrated by Shaun Tan, shortlisted for the Children's Book Council Picture Book of the Year Award 1999.

John now runs writing camps for young people and adults, just outside Melbourne.

Also available:

So Much to Tell You: The Play

a performance version

'In 1992 an imaginative and enterprising Melbourne school, Penleigh and Essendon Grammar, commissioned me to write and direct a short play for its students. This gave me the opportunity to do something I'd wanted for a long time: to put *So Much to Tell You* on the stage. Working with a sparky and talented cast turned out to be such an enjoyable experience that, after the production finished, I sat down and kept writing, turning the play into a full-length one.

'I've always wanted to write a play for an all-female cast. It was a constant irritation to me in my teaching days that there was so little material around for girls. I hope they can now enjoy reading and performing *So Much to Tell You: The Play*.'